at-risk

FLANNERY
O'CONNOR
AWARD
FOR
SHORT
FICTION

Nancy Zafris,
Series Editor

At-Risk

STORIES BY AMINA GAUTIER

The University of Georgia Press   Athens and London

Lyrics from "God Bless the Child," written by
Billie Holiday and Aurthur Herzog Jr., used by permission
of Edward B. Marks Music Company.

Paperback edition published in 2012 by
The University of Georgia Press
Athens, Georgia 30602
www.ugapress.org
© 2011 by Amina Gautier
All rights reserved
Designed by Mindy Basinger Hill
Set in 10.5/14.5 Minion Pro

Printed digitally in the United States of America

The Library of Congress has cataloged the
hardcover edition of this book as follows:
Gautier, Amina, 1977–
At-risk : stories / by Amina Gautier.
154 p. ; 23 cm. — (Flannery O'Connor Award for Short Fiction)
ISBN-13: 978-0-8203-3888-0 (hardcover : alk. paper)
ISBN-10: 0-8203-3888-5 (hardcover : alk. paper)
1. African American teenagers—Fiction. I. Title.
PS3607.A976A93 2011
813'.6—dc22   2011010454

Paperback ISBN-13: 978-0-8203-4439-3
ISBN-10: 0-8203-4439-7

British Library Cataloging-in-Publication Data available

contents

acknowledgments

"The Ease of Living" first appeared in *Colorado Review* and has been reprinted in *New Stories from the South: The Year's Best, 2008.*

"Afternoon Tea" first appeared in *Notre Dame Review* and is reprinted in *Notre Dame Review: The First Ten Years.*

"Pan Is Dead" first appeared in the *Chattahoochee Review.*

"Push" first appeared in the *Southern Review.*

"Boogiemen" first appeared in *Notre Dame Review.*

"Dance for Me" first appeared in *Southwest Review* and is reprinted in *Best African American Fiction 2009.*

"Girl of Wisdom" first appeared in *Kenyon Review.*

"Some Other Kind of Happiness" first appeared in *North American Review.*

"Held" first appeared in *Red Rock Review.*

"Yearn" first appeared in *African American Review.*

at-risk

the ease
of living

It was barely the summer—just the end of June—and already two teenaged boys had been killed. Jason was turning sixteen in another month, and his mother worried that he might not make it. A week after the double funeral, she cashed in all of the Series EE bonds she'd been saving since his birth and bought him a plane ticket to spend the summer with his grandfather. Distance, she believed, would keep him safe.

She waited until the day of his flight and told him over breakfast. "It's not forever," she said, polishing off her coffee. "Besides, it's a done deal." The ticket was paid for, and they both knew she couldn't afford it. He had no choice. She was taking off the afternoon to ride with him to the airport. She set the mug down and hurried out the door. She had neither finished her breakfast nor cleared the table. On the table she left a small plate holding the crusts from her toast, crumbs, and dollops of jelly clinging to chipped china.

She had ruined his morning.

Usually, he couldn't wait for his mother to leave so that he could go outside and chill. His boys would appear a half hour after she'd gone, and they would have the day all to themselves. This was the time of day Jason loved. The short yellow bus had already come and taken the retarded people who lived in the middle of the block out for a day trip. The adults with jobs were at work; the others were in their homes watching talk shows and soaps. A few girls were scattered on the stoops up and down the block, braiding hair and giggling at nothing. All the boys dumb enough or lucky enough to get summer jobs were out somewhere, supervising kids running through sprays of water, price checking the produce and bagging the eggs separately, or flipping burgers and asking if you wanted fries with that. But not him. Not him and his boys. They had the whole summer to themselves. They could ride down to Coney Island if they wanted. They could go downtown to the movies and sit in the Metropolitan or the Duffield all day to make up for the lack of air-conditioning in their homes. They could each buy one ticket then sneak into as many different shows as they could manage until the evening brought cooler breezes and they could go home once more. Or they could go to the park and watch the girls run around the track in those tiny blue shorts with the white trim. Or they could go to the pool and jump in the deep end with their shorts and sneakers on, dunking all the girls who had slighted them and messing up their hair. They could do anything they wanted. They could even just sit out there on the stoop all day long smoking blunts and saying whatever came to mind. He liked that best of all, but now he had to leave it. He would miss it, the times that couldn't be pinpointed to a specific action, the times that were as numerous as the days of summer vacation, when he didn't have to think about school or listen to the things his mother said or accept that the deaths of his two friends meant that nothing would ever be the same again.

"Hey yo!" a voice called up to his window.

He pulled out his duffel bag and threw it on the bed. Then he went to the window. He stuck his head out and called, "Be down in a minute!"

He didn't know anything about the South or its weather, so he didn't know what to take and what to leave. His Timberlands, of course, would go. He didn't need to pack them; they were already on his feet. His favorite baseball cap with the brim broken in half to shade his eyes. His basketball jerseys—Jordan, Ewing, and Starks. His Walkman. His favorite mixed tapes. His clippers so that he could stay smooth. His wave cap and brush. His underwear, socks, and toiletries. The overalls he had gotten his name spray-painted on at the Albee Square Mall. A stack of T-shirts, another stack of jean shorts. A tiny vial of scented oil he'd bought off a Muslim in the street. Everything he needed fit into one bag.

They were crowded in on his stoop—four boys with blunts and a forty. A dark stain of liquid made an uneven circle on the bottom step of the stoop, where they had already tipped the forty to Kiki's and Stephen's memories. Three weeks ago, they had all attended the double funeral. Now, they passed the forty, quickly demolishing it. Then they lit up.

"Took you long enough," Howie said, rising slightly to give Jason a pound. Half of Howie's hair was braided into cornrows that followed the contour of his head and then ended in tails at the back of his neck; the other half of his head was wild, where he had picked the braids loose.

"I'm here now, right?" Jason said.

"What, you was sleeping or something?" Smalls asked.

"Nah," Jason said.

"You wasn't—I mean—you know," Dawud said, making obscene hand gestures.

"No," Jason said, "I got your girl Tanya for that." Then he told them he was leaving for Tallahassee in a few hours to spend the summer with his grandfather.

"Damn," they all said at once, shrinking away from him as if he had a disease.

"Florida," said Howie. "And not even Miami, where all the honeys are. That's the South for real."

The package of E-Z Widers came out for those who didn't have blunts.

Smalls and Justice were seated on the same step. Justice laughed. "Man, you still rolling them little things?"

"Shut the fuck up, nigga. This shit is better than nothing like my man over here." Smalls pointed at Jason.

Howie said, "That's all right. I got him. It's his last day and shit. He know I got him. Right, son?" Howie passed Jason the blunt. Jason took it and lost himself in it, focusing only on getting high one last time before he left.

Smalls said, "Damn! Come up for air. This nigga act like he on death row or some shit."

"Damn near," Jason replied, coughing.

"Leave him alone. This might be his last blunt for a while. Who know what the fuck they smoke down there? Trees and shit. Corn husks," Dawud said.

"Nigga, you a fool," Smalls and Justice told him.

Howie pushed Jason. "Damn, nigga, pass that fucking el. I know it's your last day and all, but you can't take all that shit!"

They all laughed at him sitting there, puffing like his life depended on getting high. Then Howie asked, "Why you ain't never tell us you had you no rich grandfather?"

"He ain't rich," Jason said. Then he shrugged to show that he wasn't being defensive. That he could care less.

"Got enough money to just up and send for you," Smalls said. "He something."

"Just old," Jason said. "Bored, I guess. Lonely." His mother had paid for the ticket. He was being *sent*, not sent *for*, which made all the difference. Being sent for was a privilege, a vacation, a luxury that meant he could do what he wanted and enjoy himself. Being sent was a punishment and a threat. His mother was sending him to get him away from Howie, Dawud, Smalls, and Justice. Pure and simple, it was surveillance. A more motherly version of prison. But his boys didn't need to know that.

"You'd be lonely, too, if you was living in Hicksville, two towns over from the middle of nowhere!" Dawud said and laughed. A girl with braids roller-skated by and ignored them when they called to her.

"You gonna be down in one of them backwards towns like where all that Freddy Krueger stuff be going down. Little ass towns where people don't be locking they front doors and be knowing each other's name and be all up in your business," Howie said. "Better you than me."

"I'll be back before you know it," Jason said.

"Don't come back up here talking all that 'y'all come back now ya hear,' know what I'm saying?" Justice said.

Smalls said, "This nigga gonna be square-dancing. Talking about yee-ha!"

"Gonna be listening to some Dolly Parton. He come back and be like 'Biggie who? Tupac what?'" Dawud joked.

Smalls said, "Least they got honeys down there. You know, them big-legged cornbread-eating girls."

"Church girls," Justice said.

"*Yeah.*" They all said it.

"Good girls. Go to church on Sunday, turn you out on Monday," Howie said.

"Put a hurting on you," Smalls teased.

"Yeah, clear up all them bumps on your face. Skin be mad clear from all the play you'll be getting," Justice said.

Dawud said, "Won't know what to do with yourself. Put some in your pocket and save it for later."

"Maybe I'll just airmail some back to you niggas. Be all you ever get," Jason finally said. He had let them go on at his expense because he had the feeling he would miss them, because he knew the jokes hid the envy.

Better you than me. They had all been thinking it when Howie said it. But even if they'd wanted to, none of them could have switched places with him. His mother wasn't a crackhead. They were poor because she was raising him by herself, not because she was smoking her money up or giving it to some fool who was constantly going upside her head. Jason knew who his father was. Every once in a while he even came by whenever his mother asked him to "talk some sense into him." Many of Jason's friends had southern relatives, but none of them would ever be sent down South. He and they were different. He didn't relish the difference, but he recognized it. He didn't think it made him better; it just set him apart. And Howie and Dawud and Smalls and Justice all knew it, too.

Which is why they left him out of some things. They never asked him to walk to the store with them because they didn't want him to see them using food stamps and their sister's WIC checks. He didn't have any children either, and some of the boys his age already had two or three. He was almost sixteen, and he was still a punk. Whenever he and his boys caught the train and jumped the turnstiles, he always went second or third to let someone else get caught. Inside he turned to jelly each time while he waited to see if a police officer would come out from behind the door to the fake janitor's closet. He sold weed only to people he knew. He broke into the public pool only at night when it was all full and no one would be able to pinpoint him specifically if the cops came and broke it up. He didn't go anywhere with his boys on the first of the month if he could help it. He wasn't into robbing old ladies and their home attendants for SSI checks. He was a punk in thug's clothing and he knew it and they knew it, but they were kind enough not to say it out loud.

He was with them because there was nowhere else for him to

be. He wasn't smart; he wasn't athletic or artistic or talented in any way. He played basketball and tried to freestyle because everyone else did, but he wasn't even good enough to be mediocre at either. He had no plans and no prospects. He was a black boy without exceptional height or skill who could not ball and who could not rap, and as such, no one cared what he did or where he went or what he became, least of all himself.

He didn't talk to his mother as they sat on opposite sides of his duffel bag and let the taxi take them to the airport. She cast worried glances at his profile; he pretended not to notice.

"I'm sorry I had to do it like this," his mother said, "but you know how you are."

When he didn't answer her, she pressed her hands into the cracked leather of the seat. She was still dressed for work and she began to play with the cuffs at her wrists. "It's just the summer," she said. "Just a change of scenery. I just want you to get away from all this—this *madness* for a little while." *Madness*, she said, as if it were temporary and had only just come. As if it would not still be there waiting when he returned. As if he could come back and find out that a joke had been played and Kiki and Stephen were still alive.

She continued as if she couldn't stop. "Spend some time with your grandfather." She turned to look at him. He could feel her eyes on his face. He continued to watch Queens's fast approach as they neared the airport. "He hasn't seen you in a while and he's getting on in years. He can't move around like he used to."

To Jason, her words sounded like the plot for a made-for-TV movie. Or like those programs that cities and states were coming up with where they thought that sticking a city kid out in the country for a month would solve all of the kid's problems. He felt like an experiment.

When the cab pulled up to the curb, she didn't get out. His mother kissed him and pushed a wad of crumpled bills into his hand. She laid her moist palm against his cheek and whispered hopefully, "Maybe tonight you'll be able to get some sleep."

His grandfather's home attendant met him at the airport. She was holding up a cardboard sign with JASON printed carefully on it. Though unnecessary in the small regional airport, the sign made him feel important.

She introduced herself as Miss Charlotte. When she spoke, her voice made him think of family gatherings and holiday dinners. "I know Cal would have wanted to be here to pick you up himself, Jason," she said, "but he can't do all the things he wants anymore."

Two years ago, his grandfather had fallen in the shower and had a stroke. Jason's mother had flown down to Tallahassee to look after her father, leaving Jason with the apartment to himself for two whole weeks. He'd used that time to convince Chanelle to come over and stop playing hard to get. He had not thought of the paralysis that took over the left side of his grandfather's body. He had thought of that time as a vacation.

This was not the house his mother had grown up in. His grandfather had moved from a two-level three-bedroom house to a one-level two-bedroom home after the stroke made it difficult for him to climb the stairs. Miss Charlotte gave Jason a tour, taking him all over and through the house, showing him what she clearly thought of as the main attractions. She took him to the bathroom and pulled the shower curtain back to show him how the bathtub had been altered to fit his grandfather's special needs. "Now he won't have any more nasty falls in here," she boasted.

Jason pointed to a large silver-looking handle shaped like an up-side down U reinforced in the middle of the side of the tub. "What's that?"

"That's so he's got something solid to hold onto when he climbs in and out of the tub," Miss Charlotte said.

A small rubber mat with upraised bumps lined the bottom of the shower so that his grandfather wouldn't slip. A wide white plastic chair sat on top of the mat. It looked like more than one person could sit there. Jason lifted it up easily and set it on the small square of tiled floor in the cramped bathroom. The plastic was hard; it didn't bend or give. It was bone dry. It would have looked like something he could take to the beach if it hadn't had so many perforations in it to allow the water to run freely. Miss Charlotte explained that his grandfather had to sit to take his showers because one of his legs wasn't strong enough for him to stand long enough to shower on his own.

"That's his shower chair. I set it in the hallway to dry each time Cal is finished with it so that it won't get mildewed," she said. "You can go ahead and put that back the way you found it now."

She was about to take him to the kitchen and show him the bottle opener, which she used to keep lids loose on all of the bottles in the house, when Jason heard his grandfather's raspy voice.

"Is that you, Charlotte?"

"Coming, Cal!"

"Hurry up. I want to see him!"

"We're coming, you old goat! Keep your pants on!"

"Why don't you take them off for me, woman?"

Jason hadn't known that a woman her age could still blush. Miss Charlotte led him down the hallway to the bedrooms and apologized, "You've got to excuse his language, Jason honey."

The voice shouted, "Don't make excuses for me. I don't need them."

"Don't pay him no mind, Jason. He's pleased as punch to have you here. He's been talking about your coming the last three weeks. Cal, look at what I brought you," she said, pushing Jason forward as if he was a gift.

The overpowering smell of Ben-Gay made Jason's eyes water. The two windows in the room were both closed and the smell of the liniment mixed with the musty, stale air. The room was sparsely furnished and everything seemed to be in precise order. One lone bottle of cologne sat on the dresser next to a short hairbrush and a nail clipper. A wheelchair was positioned to the left side of the bed and the man who was his grandfather half sat and half reclined in the bed with his back against the headboard. He wore a white sleep shirt with faded blue stripes. A heavy gray blanket, the kind Jason had seen in Army-Navy stores, was spread over the bed.

"So you're here," the old man said, staring. Jason stared back, surprised to see that his grandfather's face was his own. He looked nothing like his own mother and father, and although he had seen pictures of his grandfather, he'd never noticed any resemblance. But it was here in the uncompromising features of the old man staring back at him as intently as he was staring himself, the same seal-brown skin, aggressive nostrils, bushy eyebrows that almost connected above the bridge of the nose, the same full lips and pugnacious chin.

Jason didn't like the way his grandfather talked to him. He didn't like the way the old man sat there, looking legless, as if he ended at his torso. "Yeah, I'm here," Jason said. "Where are your legs? You lose them in a war?"

His grandfather rolled his eyes. "I still have them, Youngblood, but I can only count on one. The stroke affected the left side of my body. My left leg is basically useless."

"Oh."

"I guess that's not cool enough for you."

Jason shrugged, not caring one way or the other. "Nah, it's okay."

"If it makes you feel any better, for as long as you're here, why don't you just pretend that one of my running buddies, my homeboys as you'd call it, didn't like the colors I was wearing one day or didn't like the way I rolled my joint and decided to smoke me but missed and only caught me in the leg. Is that any better?"

"Whatever," Jason said.

The old man asked, "Is it true that they shot those two boys down and killed them?"

"Calvin!" Miss Charlotte's exclamation broke the silence. "What a way to begin—"

The old man cut her off. "Well, boy?" he demanded. "Is it true?"

He knew that his grandfather knew the answer to that question. Surely his mother had told him. Surely the old man had been forewarned. His grandfather's blatant disregard angered him. His mother carefully stepped around the issue. They had never actually discussed the death of his friends since the funeral except for a few cryptic sentences in passing. But this old man who surely must know better had no sense but to bring the subject up right away. Jason didn't know what to think, except that he would have liked nothing more than to wheel the old man out into traffic. Since the funeral, he'd felt only numb indifference; now he claimed a pleasurable anger. His palms itched to hurt the old man. His grandfather smiled as if he could read his mind, as if he welcomed the challenge. Somehow, with his sunken body, the old man managed to give the impression that he could spring at any moment and kick ass.

"Anyway. Can I use the phone? I told my mom I'd call."

Miss Charlotte called them to dinner. The chair was removed from the head of the table to accommodate his grandfather's wheelchair. The sight of his grandfather sitting there, the back of his wheelchair making him seem like a king seated on a throne, brought back the anger.

"What's for dinner? I don't know if my mom told you or not, but I don't eat squirrel or possum," Jason said. "I'm allergic."

"Boy, this is Tallahassee, not Davy Crockett's wild frontier."

"Don't y'all eat that stuff? Rabbits and deer and all?"

"Rabbits and squirrels are just as much rodents as rats. You'll never see me putting any of that anywhere near my mouth. Come here, Youngblood."

Jason rose and approached him. His grandfather began to pat Jason's chest and pockets. Jason jumped back. "Man, what you think you doing?"

His grandfather said, "Checking for weapons."

"You're crazy. I ain't carrying nothing."

"You gonna get in my car and go do some drive-bys? Or maybe sell me some drugs? Or are you gonna wait till I'm good and asleep and then steal my basketball sneakers to sell on the corner?" his grandfather asked.

"What are you talking about?"

"You want to indulge in stereotypes, I can oblige you. Now sit down."

Jason sat. He shook his head. "You need to stop watching rap videos. It's not all like that up there."

He had begun to eat when his grandfather's hand shot out and grabbed his wrist, applying pressure. "We give thanks for our food before we eat it," his grandfather said quietly.

"I don't do church."

"Then just be still while I say something over the food."

The boy thought about it. He could refuse. This man was not his father, he didn't have to obey him. But the pressure of his grandfather's good arm told the story of strength. Veins, thick and prominent straining from knuckle to wrist, reminded Jason that this was the same man who could split a watermelon as easily as a head, the same man who had snapped the necks of chickens, blown the heads off rattlesnakes, and torn the hide off his mother's behind when she misbehaved. Jason released his fork.

His grandfather and Miss Charlotte bowed their heads.

"Lord, I don't have much, but I thank you for what I have been given. Please bless this meal and all who come under this roof. Bless us all with a nourishing meal and a good night's sleep."

Jason refused to look up when his grandfather mentioned sleep. He waited until his grandfather began to eat, then he followed suit. After some time, his grandfather spoke again.

"You play any sports, boy?"

"Nah, not really."

"Watch any?"

"Just basketball," he said.

"Who do you like? Bird? Johnson? Thomas?"

Jason thought of Michael Jordan's Gatorade commercial with everyone singing "I wanna be like Mike." What he wouldn't give to be like Michael Jordan, have Michael Jordan's money, his skill, his arrogance and confidence, his nobody-can-touch-me bravado. What he wouldn't give to linger in the air like he was free from all restraints, switch hands middunk, and keep everyone constantly guessing, constantly watching, waiting for his next move, hanging on him, all eyes reflecting his image so that he saw himself wherever he went. What else was there for him if he didn't want to be like Mike? All of his friends wanted to ball or rap. No one believed in school anymore. It was just a free version of day care. Just a place to contain society's knuckleheads and keep them off the streets for a few hours. In school, he was expected only to pass the tests that would move him into the next grade. He was supposed to memorize, regurgitate, and repeat. He was not supposed to think. All of the students who could think had been weeded out and parceled into magnet schools, gotten scholarships or vouchers to private and boarding schools, or tested into Brooklyn Tech, Bronx Science, or Stuyvesant. He and his friends were leftovers.

He said only, "I like Jordan. He's nice on the court."

"I always wanted to be Satchel Paige myself. Or Jackie Robinson."

The boy looked confused.

"Baseball," his grandfather said. "Don't look at me all cross-eyed like that. Don't stay up too late. We get up early around here. No exceptions."

"What are we gonna do? Milk the cows? Go fishing or something?"

"Boy, you've been watching too much TV."

He dreamed the first night. He was back in Brooklyn, back on his stoop. Howie, Smalls, Dawud, and Justice weren't there, but Kiki and Stephen were. They were sitting at the top of the stoop, and Stephen was holding a forty. Stephen and Kiki rose and gave him a pound when they saw him. Kiki took the bottle from Stephen and twisted the cap off. He tipped the bottle and poured the first few drops onto the concrete stoop. Kiki said, "This is for you, son," and Jason woke up covered in sweat.

By night, Jason dreamed, unless he could manage to stay awake. By day, he avoided his grandfather, spending the bulk of his time holed up in his room, listening to music and trying hard not to fall asleep. Sometimes he wandered outside, looking for something to do. He wore his headphones throughout the house, listening to his music. When his batteries ran down and he had to recharge them, he watched television. Music videos and stand-up comedy if he had the living room to himself. He pretended that he lived alone, maneuvering around Miss Charlotte and his grandfather as if they were furniture. There was nothing to do in his grandfather's house. Nowhere to go and nothing to see. Watching TV wasn't the same when there was no reason to turn the volume all the way up. His grandfather's street was quiet. There were no noises to silence and ignore. There was just him and his grandfather, a man he didn't know at all.

So it went.

His grandfather gave him chores the first week he was there, saying, "It's time you started doing something to earn your keep. This here is not one of Koch's welfare hotels."

"Ain't this what you got Miss Charlotte for?" Jason asked, balking at being used for manual labor, especially when a home attendant was present.

"She's a home attendant, not a housekeeper. She just helps me do the things I need to do for my daily survival. She helps me bathe, prepares my meals, and does the food shopping. Everything else is extra. If I want the mirrors polished, the tables dusted, I have to do that myself. She's not my personal slave, you know?" his grandfather said. "Huh. I wish she was a harem girl. Then maybe me and her could have us some fun."

Jason was to polish the old man's shoes every day, even though his grandfather went out only every other day to the doctor's. His grandfather wore his good shoes all day long in the house, even though Miss Charlotte kept a pair of brand new slippers by the side of his bed. Jason had to scrub the bathtub if he was the last one to use it. And he had to sweep the long hallway and sweep the living room. He had to bring in the newspaper and wash the dishes after Miss Charlotte cooked. There was no fried food anywhere in the house. Everything was steamed, boiled, baked, or broiled. And he was responsible for dinner. Miss Charlotte cooked their breakfast and lunch and left instructions for dinner. There were certain things his grandfather could eat and certain things he couldn't. A diagram with cartoon drawings of mustard, salt, red meat, soda, ketchup, and many other foods crossed out with big black Xs was fastened to the refrigerator with a magnet. The diagram had been drawn to be cutesy. The forbidden foods all wore diabolical grins and raised eyebrows.

He also had to make both his and his grandfather's bed every day and tidy his grandfather's bedroom, which included dusting down a dresser that was never dusty. He came to hate that chore. Standing in front of that dresser, he was forced to see himself in the big wide mirror, forced to lift each item and wipe the wood beneath it to make it gleam. First the Bible, then the heavy brush with no handle, then the bottle of cologne. He always sniffed it although he meant not to. His grandfather would wheel in and check on him to make sure that he had really cleaned the dresser and Jason had to stand there with the reflection of his grandfather's head and torso next to him in the mirror, reminding him each time of whom he looked like and who he was.

The dreams were vivid but not nightmarish. He saw no bloodstained bodies. His boys had not turned into effigies or zombies. They appeared in his dreams as they had appeared in life. Kiki full of bravado and clad in the newest fashions, Stephen slightly shy and hanging back. They always met him on the stoop in front of his house. He'd never been alone with just the two of them in real life. Howie and Dawud or someone else from their crew had always been there. In Jason's dreams, Kiki held out a forty to him and Jason tipped it back and drank without thinking. Kiki and Stephen watched him, and when he wiped his mouth and handed it back, Stephen said, "You're next," and pushed him. As Jason stumbled backward off the steps, Kiki always said, "Better you than me," and Jason would wake up with his body leaning halfway out of the bed and one palm flat on the floor.

The boy and the man lived near each other but not together. His grandfather demanded his presence at meals; other than that they kept apart. Jason pretended not to notice the physical therapy sessions, where it took all of his grandfather's strength to squeeze a small red ball, where the therapist laid his grandfather's hand palm up and exercised each finger. All the therapist did was massage and rub each finger separately, then try to bend it at the joints, but his grandfather made faces as if the woman were cutting his hand off at the wrists. When it was time for the therapy, Miss Charlotte stood at his grandfather's side with her hands on his shoulders. Jason tried not to walk by the kitchen when the therapist was there. His grandfather had caught his eyes once and held him there until he felt something like guilt pouring through him. In that arrested moment in the kitchen, Jason could guess at the things his grandfather must have had to go through in his life to get him to that point in the kitchen where he could sit and quietly endure the pain, which was clearly excruciating, with a quiet acceptance that this, too, like everything else, would pass. Jason was no great student and had gotten much of the history that he learned in school mixed up. He wasn't sure how old his grandfather was; he didn't know if he had lived long enough to have fought in any of the major wars, but he guessed that just the plain simple living of getting from one day to the next might have been something like war for the old man.

He didn't like to think of the old man, but he did anyway. He wondered what his grandfather had done before he arrived, if he was intruding, if his grandfather liked being alone. He had never really thought about what it meant to be by one's self. He knew that, in coming here, he had left his mother alone for the first time, and he wondered if she was missing him, if she was lonely without him. He tried not to think about his boys at all and he barely spared Chanelle more than a passing thought. By the time he got back, she would be with somebody else, and she'd cut him with her eyes and act like she didn't even know him.

But he did think of Kiki and Stephen.

Stephen's body had worn a black suit with a tie. He'd looked as if he were dressed for graduation or picture day at school. He had looked alive. Jason hadn't wanted to get close but his mother dug her nails into his arm and made him. "Take a good look," she'd said. "Any day now, that's you."

Her prediction terrified him. She had not said "This could be you" or "See what can happen to you?" She had spoken without subjunctives and conditionals, without mercy. Her unrelenting words made him see that when it came down to it, really came down to it, there was no difference between him and the boys in his crew, even though he had tried to cultivate one. It *was* him in the casket. Any day now, it was him. He'd looked at the corpse then. No longer Stephen Townsend, his boy, his friend, his ace. Now, a black body, a black boy, a statistic, a number, as in "one less on the street," a corpse, a cadaver, an absence.

They had taken the bodies to Merritt Green. There had been no trees near the twin plots, just the hot June sun shining straight on everyone. The heat left damp circles in the armpits of his suit. He and his friends served as the pallbearers. They'd slipped on the white gloves and lifted the coffins. As they'd marched, Jason remembered things Stephen had told him about his family. He remembered Miss Townsend's own mother had passed two years earlier and now, without Stephen, she was all alone. At the funeral, she'd looked gaunt and brittle as if a strong wind could knock her over. She'd sat there so still, hands folded and head bent, that Jason wondered if she was really there or if she had just left the shell of herself. Seated in the pew behind the immediate family, Jason remarked to his mother that Miss Townsend didn't cry, and his mother said, "Maybe she's done with crying. Maybe she cried for him all the while he was living and doesn't have any tears left now that he's dead."

When it was her turn to view the body, Miss Townsend fell out on the casket, crying without sound. She cried and her eyes were terrible and her mouth opened and closed around words as if she were talking, but not a single sound came out. It had felt like a trick, like watching a favorite TV show with the sound turned all the way down. Try as he might, Jason couldn't forget that.

The day his mother told him she was sending him to see his grandfather, he'd asked how she could afford it and she told him about the savings bonds she'd been holding for him since he was a baby. "I was saving them for you to go to college," she'd said. "But if I don't get you out of here and away from them, you might never live to see the day."

The dream was different this time.

Kiki looked at him as he approached the stoop and asked, "Yo, where did you get those kicks, son?"

"I got them downtown at Dr. Jay's."

"For real? I ain't even see those the last time I was in there."

"They're brand new."

"How come I ain't see them then?"

"You were dead by the time they came out," Jason said.

Kiki and Stephen backed away as if Jason were holding a gun on them. Stephen said, "I gotta get back to my grandmother." Then he was gone, but Jason didn't see him leave.

Kiki wound his arms around the stoop's railing and pulled himself up to sit on the top rail. He motioned for Jason to join him. "At least I ain't go out like no punk. At least I went out like a man." But he hardly looked like a man at that moment with his feet hooked around the bottom railing to keep him steady.

"But you're a boy," Jason said. Then Kiki leaned backward over the railing, falling and pulling Jason with him.

Jason struggled against the arms around him that kept tightening like bands, squeezing him so that he couldn't breathe. It was like someone was pushing him into a coffin and trying to force the lid down. He couldn't see anything, only darkness. There was only a thick blinding shroud of darkness and the suffocating feel of arms.

He was being shaken. He was covered in sweat. His body felt as if it had been dipped in water. He kept hearing a voice saying, "You all right. You all right." A calm thread of sanity and assurance thrown out to him like a lifeline. He could follow the steady sound of the phrase and the voice and let them pull him back to shore, realizing that the arms were an anchor, not a snag.

He could breathe again. He felt as if he had been submerged underwater and now had to learn to breathe in the open air again. He opened his eyes and found himself half-sitting in bed, the covers pooled at his waist, his chest sweaty, his grandfather holding his shoulders and shaking him slightly. "You all right, you all right, boy," the old man continued to say, long after Jason had opened his eyes and left the dream behind.

"Do you ever stay over, Miss Charlotte?" Jason asked the next day when he found her in the kitchen and she showed no signs of leaving. She had set up the ironing board and was pressing creases into a pair of slacks.

"Sometimes when it's needed," she said. "Off the books, you know. But you're here now."

"I ain't no home attendant."

"No, but you're a body in the house," she said. "Cal's been through so much, seen so much. Now it's like he just wants to pull into himself, pull away from everybody else. Only he can't because his body won't let him. That's hard, wanting not to need anybody, but needing them anyway, even if just for the little things. I don't like leaving him alone to fend for himself. It's not that he can't do most of these things for himself because he can. It's the loneliness. People do things when they're alone that they wouldn't think of with people around."

Miss Charlotte made it sound like a bad thing, but he didn't see it that way. There were plenty of things he couldn't do while he lived with his mother, and he couldn't wait to get out and have some privacy.

"I know what you mean. Man, when I turn eighteen, I'm getting out of my mom's crib and that's my word," he said.

"What're you going to do?"

"Get up when I want. Play whatever music I want. Loud as I want. Do my thing. Don't answer to nobody. That's all I got to say. A man's got to be a man, you feel me? That's the only way I'll ever be able to get her to stop hounding me."

His grandfather's front wheel turned into the kitchen. "So she's hounding you, huh? Let me ask you something, Youngblood. Do you think it's her job to love you and take care of you?" his grandfather asked.

"We take care of each other. I help out, too, you know." His mother paid the bills and provided him with a roof over his head, but he felt they were mutually dependent on each other. He was, after all, the only man around the house. Neither his father nor grandfather was there to help out. He was the one who had to fix things without thanks, to change the lightbulbs, to throw rock salt on the snow-covered stoop when the city workers didn't come fast enough to suit her. He was the one who had to beat mice senseless with the broom, carry the groceries, and fix the storm windows and realign them back into their grooves. So yes, it was her job to love him. He had earned it, paid for it. He had not deserved to be sent away.

"Helping out is a small price to pay when somebody works to feed and dress you and keep the lights on and the cold out. It's a small price to pay for those sneakers on your feet, those jeans hanging halfway off your ass, and that little gold ball in your ear. It's a real small price to pay to have somebody watching out for you and waiting up for you when you don't even have to say thanks. No, all you have to do is tell her your whereabouts and show your face every once in a while." His grandfather looked down at his hands, running the thumbnail under the other nails to clean them. He continued to survey his nails as he talked, making Jason feel small. "Yeah, you got it real bad. Got somebody to love you and here you are complaining about the thing that's keeping you alive, keeping you from being laid out there like your little dead friends."

The old man snatched a small orange pill bottle off the counter and wheeled himself out of the kitchen.

Jason turned to Miss Charlotte. "Damn, what I do? He's been coming down on me since the moment I got here and I ain't do shit to him. The day I walked in the door he started in on me and he's always talking about my boys!"

For some reason the old man had it in for him. All he ever did was bring up the murders. Jason thought a man his grandfather's age should know better. After all, wasn't that why he had been sent here? To get away from it? To forget?

Later that day, after Miss Charlotte had gone home for the evening, Jason went to his grandfather's room. The door was wide open. The old man was seated in his wheelchair, polishing his black shoes, a chore that Jason had forgotten to complete.

"Don't lurk in the doorway, Youngblood."

"I just want you to know that I'm gonna call my mom and ask her to change my ticket so I can be up out of here. I don't know why you so mad at me when I ain't do nothing to you."

"I'm not mad at you."

"Then what's your problem?"

"What's yours?"

"I don't have one," Jason said. "I just wanna go home."

"You think everything down here is small and beneath you, but I can't see how what you have back at home is so much better. At least

I can say I have what I want. Nobody gave it to me and that means nobody can take it from me."

"Look, I ain't come in here for a lecture. I just wanted to let you know how I felt—"

His grandfather stopped him. "You ever stop to think that maybe one of those boys could have been you?"

"What?"

"That you should be grateful it wasn't you? No, you just want to jump right back in, doing what you were doing, going nowhere fast. Your mother wanted you to come down here so you could get away from all of that mess and I guess I felt sorry for you when I heard that your little friends died. Your mother thinks you got smarts. She thinks you can turn yourself around before you end up like your little friends."

"Stop saying that! You don't have the right to be talking about them all the time—"

"I have the right," his grandfather said. "Last night was not the first night I heard you."

"Huh?"

"I'm up every night you are. I hear you every time you have one of those dreams."

"No, you don't!"

"Those boys, the ones in your dreams or the ones out on the street, can only take what you give."

"Shut up! What do you do know about them? You don't know nothing about them! Don't say nothing about them! Don't say—"
He was tired of hearing about it, tired of being vigilant night and day. Each time his grandfather talked about it, it did something to him. Made it so he could barely breathe. Made it so that he felt that he was the boy in the coffin, in the suit, with no smile. As though he was the one dead, dying, and already buried. Buried alive.

He started to cry. A boy his age. Sixteen years old and crying, but he couldn't help it. He told his grandfather that they weren't even really aiming for Kiki and Stephen. That the boys who shot them didn't even know them. That it had nothing to do with them. Revenge he could understand. Revenge was cold. Calculated. Methodical. Logical. Everybody got even. But the bullets that had killed them weren't even meant for Kiki and Stephen. This thing that happened was accidental, careless. Murder. He thought his friends deserved better. Someone should have at least known who they were.

It had only gotten worse after they died. They had been used as examples. All of the young boys older than six but younger than fourteen, dressed in borrowed brown, black, and navy suits, had been led up to the caskets by relatives and been forced to look at the boys. Kiki and Stephen had become an example of what could happen to them and all other black boys that didn't stay out of the streets. The accidental part of the shooting only made the adults feel that much more justified. The adults whispered that bullets didn't have anyone's names written on them, the phrase he'd heard on nights after a shooting when his whole block turned off their lights and pulled their shades and closed their windows to repel the stray bullets. Because it was a funeral and the dead boys' mothers were present, the adults kept the other words under their tongues. *Serves them right*, they wanted to say. Jason knew that they all believed it was just desserts just because of the people Kiki and Stephen knew and hung out with. *Sooner or later something like this was bound to happen*, they wanted to say. He knew the adults felt the same way about him. They kept their distance when he walked down the block. No one ever gave him a five dollar bill and asked him to run to the store for them. No one ever asked him to help carry a shopping cart up the fourteen steps of the stoop to their front door. To them he was the same as Kiki and Stephen, and Kiki and Stephen were the same as the boys who had shot them. So they didn't speak to him. Instead, they watched him and waited for him to die.

He told his grandfather about the shooting. Jason had never seen a boy die before. When it happened, it wasn't at all like in the movies that he and his boys sneaked into all summer long. The gun going off hadn't had the loud clap sound it has in the movies. At first Jason had mistaken the sound of the gunshots for firecrackers going off. Then the popping sounds started folks on the other end of the block to running. When the girls and the children scattered and hid he saw that Kiki and Stephen had fallen. Then the popping had stopped. Then he had run himself.

"Get yourself together," his grandfather said when he was done.

Sympathy would have shamed him, but the command released the tightness in Jason's chest, made it so he could breathe. He stopped crying, but he didn't wipe his eyes. He stood and waited to see what the old man would do.

"You can sleep in here tonight if you want," he said. "Get in."

Jason kicked his boots off and got into his grandfather's bed, just as he was, dressed in his baggy jeans and basketball jersey.

"You ought to take better care of your shoes."

The light went off. Jason heard the roll of the wheelchair as it settled on the other side of the bed and then the shuffle of a dead foot and the creak and heave of a body settling into bed. He rolled onto his back and tried to focus on the ceiling fan to keep awake, but the absence of all the night sounds he was used to and the comforting silence that remained instead were slowly claiming him. His eyelids were starting to meet when he stifled a yawn and asked, "What's it feel like, having a stroke?"

The silence was thick with his grandfather's breathing. Jason thought that he would not answer, that maybe he had asked too much.

His grandfather finally said, "You don't need to know. Settle down and go to sleep."

His grandfather's caustic response made Jason desire the answer more. "Tell me," he said. "Please. I can't sleep unless I know." As soon as he said it, he knew that it was true. He believed that he would never have a night free of wakefulness unless his grandfather told him what he wanted to know.

His grandfather said, "It feels like one half of you is gone. Like half a body is all you got left. But you still know the other half is there, you know? You can see it, this other side of your body that you're just dragging along with you, hoping that one day it's going to wake up and get started again, knowing that it won't. So you have to pretend that something can be done with it since you can't just cut it all off. It feels like having somebody you don't like coming to eat supper with you every night, and then that person has to make a big deal of the fact that he's there, so a man can't enjoy some peace and quiet with his meal. No, this person has just got to keep reminding everybody he's there."

"You talking about me?"

"No, son. That's what it feels like when you can't use a part of your body. Anybody that tells you it don't feel like nothing or they don't notice it anymore is lying. It never goes away."

"So then what?" Jason asked. He thought that there must be some secret and that the old man must have it, something that told him how to do it, how to live, how to survive, how to make it through another day when half of him was dead and dragging by his side. "I mean, what do you *do*?"

"Nothing to do. Nothing but live with it."

"I guess that's not so bad," he said. "I mean, it doesn't sound so hard."

"Who told you that?" The boy felt his grandfather shift in the bed, felt him looking at him through the darkness. "Living ain't easy. It's about the hardest thing a body can do."

Afternoon Tea

A women's organization decided to adopt the girls in our school for the year, but we weren't supposed to feel lucky. We were selected not for our scholasticism or high test marks but because our school had the highest percentage of eighth grade girls dropping out to have babies. The organization selected us out of all the other junior highs in Brooklyn as the most need-worthy, designated us as the most at-risk. Ten women from the group would serve as volunteer mentors. Time spent with the women was supposed to raise our self-esteem. It would keep us from making negative decisions that could permanently alter and impact our lives. Translation: the program would keep us from having babies at an early age and living off of welfare.

Today was the registration and the welcome for the program and my mother feared we would lose face by showing up late. She rapped on the bathroom door to get me out of the shower. "What, do you think you're a fish? Make haste!"

Once I came out, I said, "I bet this is going to be really boring."

"It will be good for you," she said. "Just give it a try. You have nothing better to do on Saturday mornings."

This was true. Most Saturdays I stayed at home alone while my mother went out. She visited our extended family, making sure they were getting acclimated to life in the States, shopping for them, and helping them barrel up goods that they wanted to send back home to Jamaica. Because she was the first to come to the States, she was the veteran, the expert, the one who helped everyone else out, the one with whom all our relatives came to live when they first moved here.

She was taking a break from visiting to accompany me to the program today.

"I still don't see why I have to go to this," I said.

She tsked at me, grabbed my shoulder, and pushed me toward my room. She ignored my question. "Hurry."

Breakfast was on the table by the time I was fully dressed. "Bun and cheese," she said. "You don't have time for anything else."

I checked my watch. "It doesn't start for another half hour."

My mother sucked air through her teeth. "On time is too late. A half hour early is right on time."

"They'll probably feed us there," I said. "I can skip breakfast. That'll save time."

My mother shook her head. "You are only to nibble while you're there. You don't want to stuff yourself on their food and look like a glutton. When people are watching, you have to make a good impression."

"Who's watching?" I mumbled as I chewed.

My mother frowned at me. "They are."

At different times, depending on whom my mother was talking about, *they* could be anyone. *They* applied to all Americans, and sometimes specifically American blacks, and on rare occasions to the family my mother had left behind in Jamaica, proud and aristocratic, constantly watching from across the sea and waiting for her to fail and go back home.

I finished off my breakfast and got up from my chair.

"What are you doing?"

"You said to hurry—"

"You'll clean up after yourself first."

"I thought we were late."

"There's always time for that," she said, watching me carefully as I took my plate to the sink and wiped the table off with a dishcloth. "You have no servants in this house."

Thirteen years ago, my mother left St. Elizabeth, Jamaica, with the seed of me inside of her, leaving behind a life of affluence for one of struggle. She had grown up a rich little girl. She'd lived in a house with servants. There were women whose job it was to cook and serve dinner, and these women were different from the ones who gathered the laundry and washed her unmentionables. Now my mother worked in a hospital five days a week, changing bedpans and dealing with other people's filth.

Twenty-two of us girls showed up at the school's library with our mothers. Ten black American women, all dressed impeccably in blue and red, waited for us. Three women met us at the door.

"Good morning."

"We're so glad you could make it."

"Please sign in at the table to your right."

They rushed to greet us, all speaking at once, then checked our names against their list to make sure we weren't crashers. Another group of three stood behind a long table loaded with red and blue gift bags. The last group of three poured cups of juice and lined them up on another table, next to plates piled high with cinnamon rolls and bagels. One woman stood apart from the others, watching and nodding as we entered and sat nervously.

"Why are they all dressed alike?" I whispered as my mother led the way to an empty table.

"They're a sorority," my mother said, pointing to the coat of arms on the colorful banner the women had strewn between two scarred bookshelves. Our library had been redone, transformed by these women and their presence. "Those are their colors."

"What about those?" Each woman wore a gold pin with indecipherable symbols above her left breast.

"They're Greek letters," she said, surprising me with her knowledge. My mother was a woman of many secrets. She knew many things but told me only what she thought I needed to know at any given moment. When I was old enough to notice that other kids had fathers and I didn't and I asked her what my father was like, my mother gave the briefest of descriptions. "He was big like so," she said, stretching her hand over her head, describing a man anywhere between five four and seven feet tall. "And black like so," she said, pointing to the darkest object near at hand. No matter how many times I asked for more, her descriptions never went beyond this. I was never to know from her if he ever laughed, if he was stingy or carefree with his money, or even how they met. In describing my father as big and black, she told me all she thought I needed to know.

The one woman who stood apart, the leader, went around the room, pumping all of our hands vigorously. She introduced herself as Miss Diane. Then she introduced the other women. Each one came forth and said a little about what she did. The women were engineers, physicians, computer specialists, lawyers, and scientists. They gave us a history of their sorority, Zeta Alpha Delta. We all rose as they sang their sorority's hymn.

My mother took pains to tuck her skirt beneath her as she sat back down on the small chair. These women, dressed in their elegant color-coordinated suits and pins, put our own mothers, dressed in their best, to shame. As Miss Diane explained the program to our mothers, thanking them for bringing us and saying that we would benefit from additional positive female role models at this crucial stage of our development, I listened and heard what sounded like a death knell to me. During these times together, we would focus on math, science, critical thinking, and writing skills, but they would make sure to cover the niceties as well, teaching us etiquette, hygiene, and grooming. We wouldn't have to pay for anything. We were to spend two Saturdays a month with them from ten until one for the remainder of the school year.

As Miss Diane talked, the other nine women circulated the tables, handing each girl a gift bag to thank us for coming. When I was handed mine, I looked at the other girls at the tables near me. Some of them I already knew, most I didn't. We were all wearing the same expression, a combination of fear, awe, and distrust. Although the ladies didn't say it out loud, their message was clear: they wanted to keep us from becoming the kind of women they would shudder to see. They wanted to save us from ourselves. The girl directly across the table from me caught my attention and whispered, "Who they supposed to be?" She was my age and American, with bad skin. We were classmates, but I couldn't recall her name. Besides the red eruptions of pustules on her brown cheeks and forehead, nothing about her looked crucial to me.

My mother pushed her way to the front of the room while other parents were gathering their coats and bags to leave. "I think this will be a wonderful program for my daughter," she said. "She wants to be a doctor. She comes from a long line of doctors. Her grandfather and her uncle both practiced medicine in Jamaica."

I hated the sight of blood, and needles terrified me. I wanted to be a librarian, to live a quiet and orderly life. To walk among stacks of silent shelves, to know every book by its number and let no book go astray. I loved to read worn books, dog-eared by people who had loved them. I wondered why she was lying. I tried to stand apart from her, to disappear each time she gestured to me, saying, "This is my daughter, Dorothy. She's a good girl. Smart."

You could tell that my mother was from the Caribbean. Even though her accent was almost completely gone, eroded away through the years, her foreignness appeared in phrases and on the ends of certain words, like my name. In school I was Dorothy, at home *Dorotee*. I absorbed my mother's sounds and phrases, but didn't repeat them. Her way of talking sounded more natural to me than the everyday language I heard outside of our home, but in her voice I heard an act of erasure, a code embedded in the words she couldn't rid of her special pronunciation. I heard in those words a warning not to repeat them. Her words told me *Don't*.

"Come," she said to me. I walked to her side, towering over her. I had to listen as she sang my praises. The women looked me over. I wondered if I looked crucial enough to them, if they saw themselves saving me from heated embraces with experienced boys, or if they could tell that I was always one of the last to be asked to dance at a house party. I was almost thirteen, but I might as well have been ten for all of my experience. I had never been kissed. Never attended a sleepover. Never done anything that did not have my mother's hand in it. Like my mother said, I was a good girl. I didn't see myself as being in a crucial stage, although I liked the way it sounded. *Crucial stage*. It was as if I was on the brink of something, standing with one toe at the edge of a cliff. At any moment I could plummet off the edge or be sharply pulled back in. Crucial. It meant I was one step away from my complete destruction. The slightest false move and I was done for. It gave my life an added sense of desperation that I liked immensely and didn't want these women to take from me. And if I were truly on the brink of something terrible, it was arrogant of them to think that they could save me.

"What was all that for?" I asked as we made our way out of the school and walked home.

"Just making sure they know who you are," my mother said. "Who you know is important. These women here can take you far."

I didn't say anything else as we walked home. My mother had already made up her mind, and so there would be no getting out of the program. I watched her as she walked slightly ahead of me, swinging my gift bag in her right hand.

Leon was out emptying his garbage. He waved us over when he spotted us. We lived three blocks away from the school, on a street populated by other West Indians, and Leon owned the Laundromat on our street. His Laundromat was more than a place to wash clothes. It was a place to buy phone cards and key chains, a place to ship goods. Twice a year, my mother bought two barrels and loaded them full of dry goods, taped them up, and sent them to relatives I'd never met.

"Where the two of you been all dressed and thing?" he asked.

"Dorothy started a program today at the school. Can't have the mothers showing up raggedy and such, eh."

"That's right now. You have to represent and show them you mean business!" he said, slamming the lid of the Dumpster down hard. "It's good to see young people with something to do to keep themselves occupied. Remember when we were that age? Our parents kept us busy. There was no lying around all day, watching TV and such. Leave you with too much time to yourself and you run around and get in trouble and all kind of mess."

"Not Dorothy. I have no worries on that account," my mother said.

"That's so," Leon said. "You doing a fine job with her."

My mother smiled modestly.

Leon was encouraged. "You sure look fine today," he said, giving her a wistful look as he grinned and showed off his gold-capped teeth.

I stood there for ten minutes while they discussed me like I was invisible, and I watched girls my age wheel their shopping carts full of dirty clothes past us and up the three steps to the Laundromat. Leon's infatuation was obvious, although my mother pretended not to notice it. I wanted to warn him about my mother, to tell him that she preferred to be left alone. There were no men in our lives. My mother's father died during my infancy and her one brother had no desire to come over. This uncle of mine now had six children, and my mother was always packing barrels full of Sweet'n Low to send to him. I had never seen my mother go out on a date, never seen her stop and smile or respond to any of the many men that expressed interest in her. Nice as he was, Leon was all wrong for her. Although he'd been living here for some time, he still seemed new.

On our first session, the Zeta Alpha Deltas showed us a video featuring "famous women of African descent." Then they gave us notebooks and asked us to write an essay about a woman of our choice who hadn't appeared in the video. When we were done, they had us read them aloud.

One by one, we each stood up and read essays about our mothers. Halfway through the eleventh essay, I could see the women's faces falling. They seemed bewildered and disappointed. Miss Diane looked as if she was going to cry.

When we were done, Miss Elaine put a hand on Miss Diane's shoulder. "I don't think they understood the assignment, soror."

Miss Diane took a deep breath and stood in front of us. She seemed to be making an effort to smile. Miss Linda motioned her to sit back down and she spoke to us instead.

"Well, girls, I commend you for your efforts," she said.

Miss Tracy chimed in, "To write such beautiful essays in so little time!"

Miss Anita added, "And it's certainly encouraging to know that you all love your mothers."

Miss Diane cut them off. "Yes, it was very good. But why don't we do this? Why don't you girls take the assignment home and work on it for our next meeting?"

We all groaned aloud at the thought of another essay, but Miss Diane was undaunted. She said, "This time, try to think of women outside of your immediate sphere. Try to think of dynamic women, women who were the first of their kind ever to do something, women who broke the race and gender barriers. Women who carved a space for themselves outside the realm that people have come to think of as a woman's role. Now do you understand?" she asked us.

We all nodded. I raised my hand.

Miss Diane called on me. "Yes, Dorothy?"

"My mother was the first woman in her family to leave Jamaica and come live in the U.S."

Although I came to hate them, my mother was pleased with my Saturday sessions. She wanted me to distinguish myself from the others in my class, to stand out. She wanted to write home about me, finally to be able to use me as an example for my relatives over the sea who all thought I was lazy and spoiled. I imagined that my young cousins hated me. Here I was going to school in whatever type of clothing I chose, watching music videos until it was time for dinner, and having the time of my life, while they were forced into uniforms and still had to go to the kinds of schools where the teachers could hit you and your parents would thank them for it. Where girls who spoke to boys were fast and loose, where they didn't have time for television after school because they had chores. These were my mother's recollections of her youth growing up in St. Elizabeth, and although two decades had passed since she'd been a girl in grade school, I imagined that much had not changed.

I hated the Saturdays, but there I was session after session. My grades weren't suffering, and so I didn't see why I had to give up my Saturdays to learn how to sit, when to cross or uncross my legs, and play with knives and forks. But, like the other girls, I didn't have a choice. None of us wanted to be there. We took our frustration out by barely participating, by looking past and through the women so bent on saving us. Our mothers could make us go, but they couldn't make us like it. So we slumped in our chairs and answered in monosyllables. Of the women, we took no notice. We doodled while the Zeta Alpha Deltas talked. We smacked our gum. If we had liked each other, we would have passed notes. But we did not think of leaving or skipping out. We were all there because our mothers made us go. Because the Zeta Alpha Deltas took attendance and we couldn't cut. Because we didn't have anywhere else to be. The library surrounded us; our sounds echoed off its high ceilings. Normally, we felt crowded in there with several classes meeting at once. But with just us there, the room seemed to swallow us. We filled only two of the eight tables. We had journals to write in, but after the fiasco with the mother essays, no one ever checked them to see what we wrote.

I showed up late for one of the Saturday meetings. The girls were clustered around the tables in the library. Something was different. They weren't their usual sullen selves. No one seemed to be biding their time. Not one pair of eyes was watching the tedious movement of the minute hand on the clock at the front of the room. The girls were all whispering. A current of energy filled the room. After I hung my coat over my chair and sat down, I heard one of the girls say, "Wait until I tell my father. He'll probably go and buy a new suit."

"Who are you going to bring?" she asked me.

"To what?"

"To our tea," she said. She slid me an ivory-colored envelope from a stack off the table. While the sorority women were setting up a game for us, I opened the envelope and read the invitation. They were samples of the invitations the ladies were sending to our homes. The tea would commemorate the end of our year's program and we would all be awarded certificates for our participation. The ladies thought we would be excited about the chance to get dressed up and show off. They said the tea would give us a chance to display our social polish.

"What's the big deal about tea anyway?" I didn't understand why we needed a special event just to sit around and drink tea. Tea was what my mother and I had each day after school as we sat in the kitchen together, before we did anything else, before we turned on the TV or prepared dinner. Tea was how we settled into the evening. It was our private cozy shared intimacy.

All the eyes at my table turned on me. Four girls started talking at once.

"Duh. It's not just tea," the girl to my left said.

One girl said that it was good practice for social functions we would attend in the future.

The girl to my right said that it would be like a miniature debutante ball, only without boys.

"Rich people go to things like this all the time," the girl with the bad skin said. I could tell that they were just repeating what they'd heard before I arrived, but their enthusiasm was genuine. The women had finally gotten to them. They'd found the one activity that would make the other girls come alive. Up until the mention of the tea, our Saturdays had been boring. Each time we came, we were forced to play stupid games we hated. One of the sorority women made us play *Jeopardy!* only the questions she made up for us were all in math. Another time, we'd played bingo. Every square on the board was a fact about their sorority. Sometimes, we didn't play any silly games. We would just gather around one table, knotting and pulling embroidery floss into friendship bracelets. In February, they quizzed us on famous black inventors and scientists. Most sessions ended with them awarding some prize to the winner. Once I won a sachet made of rose-scented potpourri, which I kept in my underwear drawer long after the scent had faded.

Everyone seemed to be excited but me. Girls who were normally despondent, who didn't speak until called upon, were chattering away and making plans that included their fathers. Those that didn't have fathers were borrowing their uncles or grandfathers for the day. I was the only one in the group without someone to escort me as I made my debut. I could see it now. Each girl would make a grand entrance into the rented hall as the ladies called her name. She would leave her father momentarily as she went forward to accept her certificate; then she would return to him and take his arm as he led her to her seat. Each girl but me. I felt sick, imagining how freakish I would look that day, all dressed up with no escort. Instead of a father, I had only the barest description.

"What will our mothers do? Do they have a special role?" the girl with the bad skin asked.

Miss Diane smiled as if it pained her and said, "Your mothers will be there to support and encourage. That's an important enough role for them."

Another girl asked, "What if mine can't make it? She works weekends."

This time the leader's smile was genuine. "Then we'll just have to make do."

Fathers, or male figures, were required. Mothers were optional.

The girl with the bad skin looked at me, eyebrows raised. Neither of us was surprised. The Zeta Alpha Deltas had not been subtle in the least way about their desire to wean us from the women they didn't want us to become. They kept encouraging us to look beyond our immediate circle, to expand our definition of role model to include women who had made real contributions to the world at large. Women such as themselves.

"Are there are any more questions?" Miss Diane asked.

The girl on my left raised her hand. "Yeah. Why do you all wear blue and red all of the time?"

Miss Diane flushed with pride. She was dressed in a blue pantsuit with a red silk scarf knotted at her throat. "That's a good question, but I can't tell you the answer."

"How come?" she asked.

"Because only Zeta Alpha Deltas know the answer. These colors are symbolic to our sorority. Perhaps one day, when you're older, you'll join our organization. *Then* you can learn what the colors are all about."

The official invitation arrived a week later. My mother was in the kitchen making fried fish and festival when I dropped the stack of mail on the table.

After she read the invitation, she got on the phone and called the mothers of some of my girlfriends. Nine of the original twenty-two girls had dropped the program, and my mother now called their mothers to gloat. She didn't come right out and say that she had told them so. Instead, she predicted great things for me, of which this tea was only the first. The Zeta Alpha Deltas would take me under their wings and give me a scholarship when it was time to go to college. Once I got to college, I would pledge their sorority and be connected to all the right people for the rest of my life. Doors would open for me left and right. All because I gave them a few of my Saturdays and was willing to drink tea.

When my mother got off the phone, she announced, "You'll need a dress."

"Leave me the money, and I'll go down to Pitkin Avenue and get one," I said. I'd been picking out my clothes for the last year because she was usually too busy to go with me.

She shook her head. "Not a dress from there. It has to be A&S or Macy's."

"Okay." I shrugged. "I'll go downtown then."

"I'm going to go with you," she said, surprising me.

We took the three train downtown on a Sunday afternoon. Once inside A&S my mother passed by the Juniors section and took me straight to the dresses in Misses.

She scrutinized rack upon rack of formal gowns. All the dresses were meant for evening wear and looked expensive and uncomfortable. My mother didn't let me select any dresses, nor did she ask my preference on my choice for style, color, or length. She made her decisions silently, rubbing her thumb across one dress's material only to frown and hang it back up. She pulled dresses off their racks and held them up against the side of my body—long dresses with satin tops and velvet skirts, sequined dresses with spaghetti straps, dresses that were concoctions of lace, dresses that came with gloves, dresses with the back exposed—dresses that all seemed way too formal for an afternoon tea.

"Here, try these on," she said, pushing me into the fitting room, after narrowing her choices down to three.

I came out in them one by one, with an ever-growing sinking feeling. Not only were the dresses way too formal for my event, but also they were hard to get into and each dress cost between sixty and one hundred dollars.

"Well? What do you think?" my mother finally asked, once her choices were back on their hangers and lying across her arm. I didn't know how to tell her I thought she was making a mistake and that I needed a simpler dress.

"I don't know."

"Which do you like the best?"

None, I thought.

"What's wrong?"

"They all seem, well, kind of dressy," I said.

"Of course," my mother said.

"Just to drink tea?"

"It's much more than just tea, Dorothy," my mother said. "It's not like what we do at home."

"They cost a lot," I said.

"You get what you pay for and quality costs money," my mother said, choosing one for me when I still couldn't pick. The winner was a cream-colored dress with a satin bodice and lacy skirt that ended in long points. Once we got to the register and my mother paid, she said, "Anyway, you're worth it. This is your chance to make an impression on them."

For just such a chance my mother had been waiting, each year growing more and more frustrated and disappointed in me as I let golden opportunities to advance myself pass me by. I coveted no plum roles in school plays, won no medals at the annual field day competition in Betsy Head Park, and could not sing well enough ever to get a solo. I made good grades, but there were other students who scored higher. In short, I was adequate, and she had been despairing I would forever stay that way.

The rest of our Saturday meetings at the school were devoted to preparations for the tea. The Zeta Alpha Deltas were using the tea as a chance to teach us how to put on a social program, and so we spent our three hours learning about hall rentals, going over seating charts, ordering flowers, debating band choices and menu selections. They wanted us involved in every aspect of the planning. The day of the tea, we were supposed to show up two hours early in our work clothes to set up the room. As the tea drew nearer, it was all the other girls could talk about, and images of my own father haunted me.

Neither my mother nor I had yet to mention what I could do since I didn't have a father to escort me. When I finally reminded her, she said, "We have more than enough family. I'll find you a father. No worries."

I didn't want a substitute father. I wanted my own. Or at least enough information about him so that I could re-create him and pretend, but my mother lived in a private world of memories she did not share.

I know he must have been handsome for my mother to love him. Handsome and big with very black skin. This is as much as my mother has told me, but not as much as I know. I pieced together images of him from what I knew of her. She wouldn't have liked him at first. It wasn't her way. She must have met him and loved him against her will. She wanted to love a safe man, preferably an older one that didn't have many demands. She wanted to bear children, cook meals, keep house, and be left in peace. She wanted something simpler than what she'd grown up with. She didn't want servants around her or a house that took more than two people to clean it. She wanted comfort, but not luxury. My father must not have been any of these things. She couldn't know that I often wondered about him. I didn't even know if he still lived in Jamaica. It seemed most likely that he never knew about me. My mother left her family's country home for America when she was two months pregnant with me. I never understood why she left him, but I guessed it was because he had the power to make her change her mind.

Still, she must have suspected that something like me could come about. Used to being protected and cosseted her whole life, she must have thought herself immune and panicked upon realizing that her body was just as human as every other woman's. I used to fantasize that my father had been one of the servants in my grandparents' house. I imagined feverish and clandestine meetings between my mother and him in closets and bathrooms. It wasn't until I got older that I realized it would have been impossible for her to love him had she met him in her home. For the most part, my mother was a proper girl. Raised in a house with servants her whole life, she would have no more noticed one than she would the wallpaper, let alone run off with one or let one drive her out of her country. Unlike here in the States, where we were all lumped together regardless of status, there class made a world of difference. Kinsmen or not, in those days, he would have been beneath her.

My mother didn't say anything else about the tea. Whenever I asked her if she'd found someone, she told me not to worry.

The night before the tea, she came home from work excited. "I finally found a father for you!" she said.

"Who?" I asked between mouthfuls. I had microwaved the previous night's escovitch fish and started eating dinner without her.

"Leon!"

I almost choked. There was my mother, standing before me, telling me that she'd gotten the laundry man to pretend to be my father, looking at me like I should be happy. She said he would meet me there. I could see it now. The other girls would laugh me right out of our rented hall.

"Leon?" I asked. I had been secretly hoping that she wouldn't find anyone and I wouldn't have to go. I hated taking pictures and being looked at. "What happened to all of our family?"

Everyone was busy that day, she said, or else too young or too old to pass for my father.

"He's not even related to us," I said. "We don't even look alike."

"You don't resemble your father anyway, except for the height. You look most like me."

I wondered if Leon had a real suit, or if he would just throw a blazer over his outdated jeans. Years ago, it had been the style to have artwork spray-painted and graffitied on the front and back pants legs of jeans. The fad had come and gone but Leon still wore his. Every other day, he wore a pair of stone-washed blue jeans with Mickey Mouse or Donald Duck spray-painted onto the legs. He would embarrass me with his tight jeans and his gold teeth. "But people will see. Everybody will see us!"

"And so?" my mother said. "Leon's a hard-working man and he's always been good to us." Her focus on class had gradually eroded but I wasn't as accepting as my mother. Leon was nice enough, but I didn't want anyone to believe he was my father. Not Leon with his outdated jeans and his camel suede shoes and his loud patchwork shirts in multicolors. He was everything I was trying not to be.

"But Mommy, he's so—"

She made a sucking sound with her teeth to silence me. "Hush. What's done is done. I already invited him and he said yes. I can't take it back now. Besides, it's only for the one day, Dorothy."

My mother waited silently for me to nod or do anything to show that I agreed, but I remained still. We had never had an argument before. I had never talked back, disobeyed, or sassed her before. Neither of us knew what to do now.

By an unspoken agreement, we didn't yell. Instead, we retreated into separate corners of the kitchen, fighting with brooding silence. In the silence between us, my mother began to make our tea, lashing me with her careful, studied indifference. She had no words for me. My mother's anger hung in the air. In the clang of stainless steel against aluminum as she fitted the opened neck of the kettle to the faucet as if choking it. In the kettle she filled and banged down on the burner. In the three clicks it took before the gas came on. In the hiss of the tiny beads of water at the spout as they evaporated into the heat of the flames.

When the water was ready, I fought back with my own sounds.

The accidental slam of the cabinet door after I'd pulled down my cup. The dull clanging of my silver spoon hitting the ceramic bottom of the cup as I stirred too hard. The spill of sugar into my cup as I made my tea just the way I liked it—too too sweet—and dared her to say something.

The day of the tea, I showered, dressed in street clothes, and wrapped a scarf around my head to keep my hairstyle in place. I took my new dress and put it into a bag, along with my shoes and stockings, and headed out the door.

I passed the Laundromat when I turned the corner. Leon was open early this Saturday. He was bent over in the doorway, sweeping dust from the welcome mat. On either side of him, by the door, there were barrels and barrels waiting to be sold and shipped. I wished, for the moment, that I could climb into one and hide, that someone would seal me up and send me far away, that the ceremony could go on without me.

I walked quickly by before he could see me and caught the three train at Saratoga. I didn't switch to the four at Utica like I should have. I didn't know exactly what I was doing, but I got off at Grand Army Plaza, a stop that wasn't mine. I don't remember doing it on purpose, but I found myself far from where I was supposed to be.

There was a small Caribbean store on the corner by the train station. I went in and ordered a beef patty and a cola champagne and took it to one of the three small tables in the back. It was early still yet and not many people were in the store. No one bothered me as I sat in the back and ate the flaky yellow patty and tried to make myself disappear.

I never showed up for the tea.

Later, I would regret this act of rebellion. On college campuses, I would see sorority women like the ones who tried to mentor me. I would go to their step shows and social programs, watching them hungrily as they all dressed alike and wore the same colors and melded into each other, distinguished only by their hair styles. I would see them pass each other on campus and call out special greetings, see them cluster together in lines in the cafeteria, see them never being alone. And I would think of how I missed my chance to know their secret ways, how I had closed myself out. I would watch them as if through a window of thick glass and I would want to break through and get in. But for now, I was satisfied to thwart their attempts to mold me into someone else.

I sat in my corner of the shop and I imagined the other girls in their finery being led into the banquet hall on the arms of their tall and strong fathers or grandfathers and thought of how I had no one. I blamed my father, whom I had never met. I didn't blame him for leaving us because he hadn't known about me. I blamed him for loving my mother in the first place, for loving her so much and so hard that she felt compelled to flee him across an ocean. I blamed him for forcing us to be alone, for leaving my mother emotionally paralyzed, scared to meet another man because she might find that same intensity again, the kind that could take her away from herself, and scared to meet another man because she might not. Had it not been for that, I could have had another father. There were plenty of men willing enough. They flocked to my mother wherever we went. They watched her as she carried bags, knowing she would not allow them to help. I watched them eye her when we rode the subways and buses, and whenever we went to visit relatives, there was always a new man, a friend of so-and-so's waiting hopefully to be introduced. But she would not entertain any man's company. And I was left with Leon.

I killed the hours in the back of that tiny shop. The woman at the counter didn't bother me. After I finished my patty I bought a bun and cheese and played with it. I wasn't ready to go home just yet, but eventually I would have to face her. I didn't know if my mother was still at the rented hall, out somewhere looking for me, or already home and waiting. I had no idea what would happen between us when I finally made it back.

But on any other day, I knew how it would be when I got home. After a day of family duties that it would never occur to her not to perform, my mother would go through the house and head for her bedroom. There she'd undress in front of the mirror, revealing herself slowly.

A tissue from a box of Kleenex would take away her outside smile, leaving her house lips in its place. She'd pick up the brush off her dresser and pull it through her hair, not one hundred times, but just enough to quell the itch in her scalp and to direct the thick, unbending hair into order. My mother would shrink in front of the mirror as her shoes came off. She wouldn't bother to get her slippers. The rest of the afternoon and evening would see her barefoot. Small curling toes with fading paint would guide her to the kitchen, where she'd fill our kettle with water and would light a flame under it. All this would be done without sound. She would have had enough in the street and in the living rooms of all the relatives she had visited. She would leave the kettle to its own devices and settle on the couch in the living room. There she'd sink into the couch as if dissolving, feeling at this moment that she could leave the world and never look back. Then my mother would think of me. First she would wonder what I was up to and hope I was minding myself. She would wonder if I was behaving well. Maybe, for one moment, she'd think of my father and wish she hadn't left him. She'd get up and walk to the kitchen to turn off the kettle. And that's where she'd be when I returned. When she heard me enter, she'd call out and ask me how my day went, and I would tell her fine.

pan is dead

Blue sent letters, begging letters, meant to soften a small space in our mother's heart. The letters were frequent, relentless, more punctual than bills. They slipped in with the gas and electric bills, the phone bill and the rent reminder, long number-ten envelopes mixed in with the short fat ones the credit card people sent. For months, Blue's letters came from a rehab center in upstate New York, all addressed to our mother. Then one came from Brooklyn addressed to my brother, Peter. Blue thought he was being slick, but our mother knew what he was doing.

"I'm supposed to believe that all of a sudden he wants to see his son? What about all those years before? He must think I'm all kinds of a fool," our mother said, finally deciding to read the last of the letters. She would have us know that she was not all kinds of a fool. She was no longer a foolish young girl willing to let Blue lead her by the nose. "I was a fool for him once and look what it got me," she said, looking at Peter.

A few days after opening the first one, our mother softened. We came home one day to find her slowly going through them. They were stacked on the kitchen tables in two piles. She didn't look up when we came in; she didn't even notice us when we turned on the TV in the living room and glued ourselves in front of it. She just sat there reading. She burst out laughing in the middle of one letter, put it down, and shook her head at it. Much later, when I turned back to look at her, I saw that she'd gone through a whole pile of Blue's letters. She was working on the second pile, her hand covering her mouth, crying silently.

After some time, she remembered us. "What do you think?" she asked Peter. "Says he's back in Brooklyn now. You want to see him? You're old enough to decide for yourself."

"I don't care," Peter said. Blue wasn't the kind of father any boy would want to claim. A high school dropout. A heroine addict, a former one if his letters could be believed. A love from our mother's wilder days, Blue belonged to our distant past. According to Peter, he used to come by regularly. By the time I was old enough to have remembered him, Blue had stopped coming. He'd gone away to nobody knew where.

"Well, he checked himself into that place all on his own. I guess that says something," our mother said.

She invited him for dinner, saying that it would do him good to spend some time with his son.

"Look at you," Blue said, when I opened the door to let him in. He showed up in denim work overalls and a lumberjack shirt, carrying a small leather bag. His overalls were covered in grease spots, his hands stained with car oil. "I remember you when you could barely walk. Cute little thing in your walker, running all over the house, tearing stuff up."

I let him in and followed behind him, hoping he would tell me more stories about myself. Blue fascinated me with his skin so black it was blue, his hands so dirty his palms were black.

"Where's your mother?" he asked, looking around hopefully.

"In the kitchen," I said. "Dinner's not ready yet."

"That's all right. I need to clean up anyway. I came straight from work," he said. "Mind if I use your bathroom?" he asked.

I pointed down the hallway. Blue took his little bag and disappeared into our bathroom.

Our mother came out of the kitchen, wiping her hands on a dishcloth. "Did I hear the door? Was that Blue?" she asked.

"Yeah."

Peter came out of his room and joined us.

"Well, where is he?" she asked me.

Peter said, "I bet he's in the *bathroom*." He said it slowly, enunciating each word. He and our mother shared a look, but all she said was, "Hmm."

Blue stayed in the bathroom over twenty minutes. Peter timed him. He was relaxed when he finally came out and sat down to eat with us. Both our mother and Peter watched him guardedly, as if waiting for him to vanish.

"So how's school?" he asked Peter.

"Don't get this boy to talking about school. We'll be here all night. That's all he do. Eat, sleep, and breathe school. Read everything he can get his hands on. I can't get him to take his head out of the books sometimes. He scores the highest out of everybody in his grade at that school. They've already skipped him twice." The way she said it was a complaint. Because he scored the highest on all the standardized tests and finished assignments in five minutes that took the other kids more than an hour, Peter was what teachers called "gifted." He'd skipped two grades, tested into an enrichment program, and was about to receive a full scholarship to a private school in Manhattan for the following year. These things did not make her proud, only perplexed. Our mother didn't like a lot of fuss. She'd wanted to raise a normal boy, not a gifted one.

"But that's good," Blue said, impressed. "It's important he gets a good education."

"You think it's good. I'd like to see how you feel when you've got to take off work to go up to his school because every time you turn around some teacher's calling you to come and get him!" she said.

"You fighting in school, boy?" Blue asked him.

"I wish," our mother answered. "That I could understand. This was a while ago, but here's one. His teacher called me up because he disagreed with her. What was it about? Remember?"

"The shortest distance between two points," Peter said, his head low over his plate.

"How's that?" Blue asked.

"She told the class that the shortest distance between two points was a straight line," Peter explained, his voice sounding tortured.

"Yeah," Blue said, as if he'd just thought of it. "It is."

"No," Peter said. "*Connecting* two points, but not *between* two points. I could draw a vertical line between two horizontal points that could go on infinitely."

"Yeah?" Blue asked, as if it was something very special.

"Never mind," Peter said.

Our mother wouldn't let it go. "And what about that book report you did that almost gave your teacher a heart attack?"

"I don't want to talk about it," Peter said. He didn't like to talk about being smart, I knew. He had told me before that he had two ways of talking: one for when he was at school and one for when he was at home.

It was just as well he didn't talk about the book report, since my mother and I never understood his explanations. Peter had gone into one of his phases. He'd picked up Ovid's *Metamorphoses* and gotten hooked on Greek mythology, reading everything he could find on the subject for nearly a month. He'd tried to pull me in with stories of Titans and Olympians, but I wouldn't let him. His favorite was Pan, the god of shepherds and flocks. He'd tried to tell me that Pan's death was a matter of belief, that he died simply because everyone heard and repeated that he had, and that his death signaled the birth of Christianity in the classical world, but Peter succeeded only in scaring me with his facts. I didn't want to know the things my brother knew.

"See?" our mother said. "I've got to deal with this day in and out. They're about to give him an award in three weeks."

"I still say that's good," Blue said. "Don't think you got those brains only from your mother's side. Smarts run on my side of the family, too, you know."

"What was it like up there in rehab?" Peter asked. Our mother shook her head at him, but he ignored her. "Was it hard?"

Blue didn't seem to mind. "A lot of talking. All these meetings where they made you talk all the time. Tell your story again and again. How and why you got there. A lot of church, too. They took attendance at the Sunday service. So you had to be there. Or else you lost your bed."

"What else?" Peter asked. I kicked him under the table.

"Breathalyzers at night when you came in for curfews. If you missed curfew they put you out," he said. He snapped his fingers. "Just like that."

"Sometimes people deserve to be put out so they can understand what they used to have," our mother said. "That's the only way they appreciate anything."

"That's the truth if I ever heard it." Blue shook his head and put his knife and fork down. "You know, when you want something, you can't always just reach out and take it," Blue said. He looked over our heads to our mother, talking only to her. "You got to work hard for it. Then again, sooner or later, it might just fall into your lap."

"You sure got a lot of nerve," our mother said, smiling to show she didn't mean it.

Blue had gone and Peter and I were at the bathroom sink brushing our teeth before bed. Peter hadn't said a word since Blue left. He didn't seem to know how lucky he was to have his father back. My own father was dead and buried; I never wondered about him. He was not nearly as interesting to me as the flesh and blood Blue, the Blue who could change the people around me, the Blue who could make my brother quiet and sullen while reminding our mother how to smile.

"Blue's nice," I said. "I hope he comes back again."

Peter didn't say anything.

"What's wrong?"

"Nothing."

"There is."

"I thought he was supposed to have come for me."

"He did," I said.

"Yeah right," Peter said.

"Then what did he come for?"

He wouldn't talk.

I jabbed him with my toothbrush. "Tell me."

"You're too young."

"Am not. Tell me. Tell me. Tell me. Or else you'll have to smell me." I lifted my arms and revealed my armpits.

"You're such a baby," Peter said.

"Tell me. Tell me. Tell—"

Peter clamped his hand over my mouth. "Okay!" he said. "Just be quiet." We went to our room and he pulled out one of Blue's letters to our mother and showed it to me. It was short, just one sentence: "Deloris baby, sometimes the nights here so long it can make a man cry."

We woke one night to hear our mother at the door.

"What are you doing here at this time of night?" she asked.

It was Blue's voice. "Please, baby. Let me come in."

"Are you crazy?"

"Blue's here," I said, excited. I began to crawl out of my bed.

"Get back in the bed," Peter commanded from his top bunk.

"But—"

"Shh!" he said. "Listen."

We heard our mother saying something about it not being right with us asleep in the house.

Then Blue: "Deloris, please. I got to come in. I can't be out there tonight. I need help. If you don't help me Deloris, I won't make it. Just let me stay. I'll sleep on the floor. Don't let me go back out there tonight." He sounded like he was crying.

"I can't."

Blue said, "Come on, Deloris. You used to love me, baby. You know it." He crooned, "Deloris, youuuu used to looovvve me, giir-rlllllll."

When we woke up the next morning, Blue was fast asleep on a heap of oily blankets on the living room floor.

"It's not right to kick somebody when they're trying" was all our mother said.

Blue began to stay with us. He would come to our house with oil-stained clothes. Sometimes there were perfectly round holes in his jeans from where the chemicals that leaked on him from under the cars had eaten all the way through the material. Once a week, he had to buy some sort of corn husker liquid to clean the layers and layers of grease and oil caked on his hands. During the day, he was at his old job working on cars. In the evenings, he was with us, making our mother laugh once again. He was able to bring something out in her we'd never seen. Something that softened her. Blue brought bottles of Grey Goose or B&B and he and our mother would sit in the living room, drinking. Occasionally, we could hear their laughter as we drifted off to sleep.

Before she'd ever met my father, our mother had loved Blue. Another woman she had been. A medical assistant who smuggled free hypodermics out to her boyfriend, because although she didn't like his shooting up, she wanted him to be safe. A young woman strutting past the junkyard where he worked, wearing halter tops and Sergio Valente pedal pushers to catch his eye, hoping he'd stop her to talk.

The three of us were working on a thousand-piece jigsaw puzzle one rainy afternoon two weeks later when Blue asked us nervously, "Is it cold in here?"

"I'm fine," Peter said.

"Me too," I said, but I saw Blue shiver.

"Come on, let's go for a ride," he said.

Blue drove us down Atlantic Avenue under the train tracks. Small drops of water from the tracks sprayed down across the car window. We were framed on both sides by the rusty steel posts, and everything looked the same, but Blue seemed to know where to stop.

"Wait right here," he said. "I'll be right back." He jumped out of his side and slammed the door behind him, walking at a fast pace, heading toward a shadowy figure standing on the corner a block away.

"Blue must know that guy," I said, watching as he slowed when he got to the man's side. Their profiles talked to each other. Blue put his hand out, maybe to shake. "See, look. They're shaking hands."

"No they're not."

"Yes they are. See."

"Shut up," Peter said.

The other guy took his hand and they stood like that for a second, with their hands in each other's. Then they drew back, and Blue walked away from the man, turning the corner, where we could no longer see him.

Every five minutes, I asked Peter what time it was, but Blue didn't come back.

"Where did Blue go?" I asked.

Peter shrugged, silent and distant. He was hugging himself like it was cold.

"What if he never comes for us?"

"He will. And when he comes back, he'll be feeling fine."

"How come?"

For a while, he wouldn't say anything to me. He started to play with the radio. He shut it off and began to open and close the glove compartment, pulling it down and slamming it closed hard. Then in a small voice, "You don't understand anything."

"We're never going to get back home," I said, trying not to cry.

Peter flicked a glance to me. "You're with me," Peter said. "Remember that." He put his arm around me. We sat like that for about twenty minutes, scared.

When Blue came back, he was walking much slower. He seemed to walk and dip, his head nodding. He opened the driver's door. "Hey," he said, smiling easy at us before getting in. "How y'all doing?"

Peter didn't answer. I didn't know what to say.

Blue seemed different from when he left. Looser, somehow. He looked happy and sleepy.

"Everybody all right?" he asked, scratching his knee.

Peter wouldn't talk.

"We're fine," I said.

"Good. Yeah, that's real good," Blue said, and he drove us home.

"Where were you?" was the first thing our mother wanted to know when we got back.

"Hey baby," Blue drawled. "I just took them for a little ride. I wanted to spend some time with my son and I didn't want to leave the little miss all alone."

Our mother looked straight through him. She yanked us over to her side. "You got a lot of nerve," she hissed. "I should kill you dead!"

"What's wrong, Deloris baby? What you talking about, girl?"

"Don't try to play me for a fool, Blue. I know you. I know you," she said. "Whatever you do, you gonna have to do it on your own."

"Come on now," Blue said, smiling easy. "I was just spending some time with my son."

"You can do that right here in the house, Blue. I never gave you permission to take them nowhere. I never said you could do that."

"You never said I couldn't," he said. "Come on baby, what's the matter baby?"

"Don't play with words with me when I'm this close—" she stopped and looked down at us. Then she did something she hardly did. She put her arms around us. "You all right?" she asked us, her hands warm on our shoulders. I didn't answer. I wanted the feeling to last. I thought it felt familiar. She must have touched us like this before—with love and concern and tenderness—but I couldn't remember that far back.

"We're okay," Peter said, cutting the moment short.

Her hands slipped away and she straightened her shoulders. "Good. What happened?" she asked us. "Somebody is going to tell me something."

"Nothing," Blue answered. "Come on, now. It's cool. Hey."

Our mother looked at Peter. He didn't answer.

I did. "Blue got out of the car and he met a man and he shook his hand and then he—" Peter pushed the back of my knee in with his and I stopped talking.

"Shaking hands? What is she talking about?" our mother asked.

"Just an old friend I ran into," Blue said, watching us. "Nothing happened, baby."

Our mother didn't know what to believe.

"Nothing happened," Peter finally said. "We just went for a ride. That's all." Then he went to our room.

Our mother wore a borrowed dress the day of the awards banquet. A mixture of royal blue and black, with four panels that intersected at her waist, held together by a thin black strip of a belt, cut low in both front and back. The dress looked as if meant for dancing, for spins and turns, whirls and dips, not for an awards ceremony. "How do I look?" she asked, pirouetting in the living room, making the panels fly. She was more than a little drunk; she and Blue had killed a bottle of Grey Goose an hour earlier.

"You look nice," I said.

"If looks could kill, baby!" Blue said, clapping and whistling.

"What do you think?" she asked Peter.

"We're going to be late if we don't leave now," he said, pulling on his suit jacket and leading the way out.

When we arrived and gave Peter's name, they treated us like royalty. The woman at the table consulted a seating chart, then looked up at us with a bright smile. "Oh yes, our scholarship recipient," she said. She sent one of the hostesses into the room to tell them we were here. Then she embraced Peter as if he were her own son. "We've got a special table up front just for you and your guests."

"His guests," our mother whispered to Blue. "How's that for something?"

The first woman handed us to a different woman. She was statuesque, dressed in one of those voluminous dresses that seemed to have no arms or sleeves yet managed to flow over her arms to her wrists like the wings of a dove sweeping down. "Here you are!" she said to Peter, leaning down to hug and kiss him, leaving a lipstick mark on his cheek. Shaking Blue's hand, she turned to us and said, "This must be your lovely family." She leaned down to me, managing to smile widely and talk through her teeth at the same time, and said, "You've got a tough act to follow, miss. But we know it must run in the family."

Then she stood up to meet our mother and kissed her on both cheeks. "And you—you must be so proud." Then she led Peter away with her, stopping every few minutes to introduce him to someone. Her pride in him was clear. Her arm never left his shoulder.

We followed a hostess to our table. For the first half of the ceremony, Peter sat at the dais table, his face blocked by a pitcher of unsweetened iced tea and a vase of fresh-cut flowers. Once the meal was served, he joined us.

"You ever see anything like this before?" our mother asked.

All of the tables wore skirts. The carpet matched the chairs and drapes. A silver place holder sat in the middle of the table, a rectangular white square nestled securely within it, announcing that our table was reserved.

Blue watched the well-dressed hostesses. "There's more gold in here than in Fort Knox."

We sat down to plates of salad and we poured our dressing from a bowl like Aladdin's lamp. Each guest had more silverware and china than I'd ever seen. Three different glasses, four spoons, two forks, two knives, a coffee cup and saucer.

Sometime during the meal and all of the speeches, our mother began to slouch in her seat and sit sideways, propping her feet in Blue's lap. More than a few people stared. She ignored them and looked at Peter. "How come you're not eating?"

"I'm not hungry," he said.

"I'll help you out. I can finish that for you," Blue said. Our mother waved him off.

"You better eat it," she said. "Nobody is playing with you."

"This food is nasty," Peter said, pushing the plate farther away.

"What are you talking about? You know how much money these people paid for these luncheon tickets? Fifty dollars!" our mother said.

Blue turned to him. "Boy, this food is not nasty; it's expensive."

"You can't make me eat it. You can't tell me what to do. You might be my father, but you're not my daddy," he said.

Blue's face fell. He looked at me, caught in the middle, but I couldn't help. I didn't know this brother, this Peter who mouthed off in public. Blue looked down at his plate and said, "I'm here now and I'm trying to be your father if you let me."

"Yeah right," Peter said. "I know you didn't come for me. I know why you're here." Our mother pulled her feet away and did her best to ignore all of us. Peter leaned closer to Blue, but I still heard him when he said, "You really think she wants a junkie like you?"

We went our separate ways when we came back from the affair. Our mother to her bedroom, and Blue to the living room. I followed Peter into our room, where I sat while I watched him kick things around for ten minutes.

Finally, he spoke to me. "Why did she have to act that way?"

"Like what?"

"Why did she have to wear that and drink all of that stuff before we left? You'd think she'd never been anywhere before. They deserve each other," he said. He turned to me. "Look at them and look at me. I'll never be able to get away from them."

"But Blue didn't do anything."

"He started this whole thing."

"Are you sorry he came back?" I asked, wondering if he would tell her now that Blue had left us in the car.

He didn't listen to me. He went to his desk and picked up one of his books on gods and demigods. "I used to think that one day she'd be proud of me," he said, idly turning the pages. "When I was older and rich and had a great job, I was going to take care of her. I was going to buy her a lot of fancy things," he said. He picked up a pencil sharpener shaped like a globe and put it back down. "Now I'm not doing anything for her. I'll just take care of you. Only you."

"How was you gonna do all that anyway?"

"I'm going to be somebody big," he told me. "Money won't be a problem."

"You gonna do what Ma says?"

"I don't want to be a doctor," he said. "But I could be a lawyer. Most presidents are lawyers first."

"Boy, you can't be president." This much I knew. Everyone knew that the president was always white and never from Brooklyn.

I left him and went to the kitchen for a glass of juice. Blue was packing in the living room. He had the same look on his face that I'd just seen on my brother's, that look of hurting and trying to hold it in.

"He didn't really mean it," I said.

"He's right," Blue said. He folded his own borrowed suit and laid it on our couch.

"You're no junkie," I said. "I've never even seen you eat a bunch of candy!"

Blue looked at me strangely, then the corners of his mouth curved. "You're right about that," he said. "Never touched the stuff. You know, I had something for him." He went to his greasy bag and pulled a small brown paper bag out of the zippered section. "I was gonna give him these." He opened the bag and showed me ten packs of green stars. "They glow in the dark," he said. "They're all in there. Planets and stars and even the moon, too. I checked."

"What are you gonna do with them now?"

"Throw them away, I guess. He's embarrassed. He's ashamed of me. He won't want them. He doesn't want anything from me." He crumpled the brown bag. "You know you can make the whole sky with them?" Blue said. "Everything."

"Can I have them?"

"You don't have to—"

"No, I want them. Please?"

Blue tried to straighten the bag out, pressing the wrinkles between his fingers. He took the packets of stars from the bag and handed them to me as if they were precious. He piled the packets into my open hands and solemnly folded my fingers, one by one, over the stack of green stars.

Peter was lying facedown on his bed when I returned. "Look what I got," I said.

"What?" He didn't even look up.

"Look." I opened my hands.

"Oh snap! Where'd you get those?" Peter asked, jumping down from his bunk.

"Blue gave them to me," I bragged. "He gave me a whole bunch. Like ten packs. They were supposed to be for you."

"For me?"

"Yeah. Don't you feel burnt?"

"Give me those," he said, snatching them from me.

"I'm telling!"

Peter ignored me. He cupped the packets in his hands and looked down at them. "These are like three dollars a pack."

"Yeah, so?"

"This must have cost him like thirty dollars."

"So?"

"In order for him to buy me this, it means he couldn't—" Peter looked up at me. "Forget it."

"Couldn't what?"

"You're too young to know," he said.

"Couldn't what? Couldn't what couldn't—"

"—He couldn't buy something else for himself, that's all."

"Something he really wanted?"

"Yeah," Peter said.

I followed him to the living room. Blue and all of his belongings were gone, his borrowed suit the only proof he'd ever been in our lives.

Two days later, Peter called me into our room. He'd been holed up in there for hours, refusing to let me in.

The room was dark. "How come the lights are out?" I asked.

"Look at that," he said.

I looked up. Blue's stars were spread across the ceiling.

"You're gonna get it," I predicted. As soon as our mother saw how he'd ruined her ceiling, he'd get a beating. He seemed not to hear me. His eyes were fixed on the ceiling, on all the tiny stars he had plastered up there. Some of them were done up like the constellations. I thought I recognized the Big Dipper. "You better not let Ma see."

"She can't hurt me," he said.

"They'll fall off soon anyway," I predicted.

"Nope," he said. His voice was barely audible, a whisper of pleasure. "They won't. They're made to last."

push

The teacher's clothes hang off her. She is what the girl's mother calls a "Skinny Minnie." Even the girl's sister dresses better. She gets her clothing from Lerner's, which has not yet become New York & Company. When the sister is away at work, the girl slides the magazines out from her sister's hiding place and stares at the models, especially the two black ones. The women are lovely in a way the girl didn't know black women could be. Her mother is not beautiful, neither is her sister, though her sister probably could be if she tried a little harder.

When the teacher calls her back after releasing the class into the schoolyard, which is a parking lot for the teachers in the morning (they have to clear their cars out after lunch to make room for the kids to play at recess), the girl does not fully grasp that she has done something wrong. The teacher lets all the other kids go and then says, "Not you."

"Did you push Colleen down the last flight of steps on the way out of the building?" Mrs. Greenberg asks in such a way that the girl thinks it entirely possible she is merely curious. After all, the stairwells are painted a deep dark green, which makes it hard to see. The girl wears thick neon laces in her Adidas and she follows her laces down the stairwell, using them as a light to keep her from crashing into the kid in front of her, unless she wants to. Colleen's place is right in front of her. They are both five feet two inches, but the girl has more hair, which makes her seem taller, so Colleen gets to stand in front. This is size order. Nothing about it ever changes. The girl thinks that nothing ever will. All day long there is a small wooden chair to sit in, with one bolt missing and one edge torn away so that whenever the girl wears tights, which is only on picture day or when her mother forces her, she gets snagged to the chair. There is always the small metal desk with the fake wooden top. It doesn't lift the way the desks do in the old movies, where the kids come to school with lunch pails and apples and where the boys attach mirrors to the front of their shoes so that they can look up girls' skirts. (Okay, the part about the mirrors and the shoes isn't from a movie. The girl's mother's boyfriend has told this story more than once, claiming it was something he'd done in his boyhood days, and the girl believes him. She has seen a picture of her mother as a schoolgirl, with a bright clean face and mischievous eyes, and has come to think that the kids in her mother's day were probably all up to something. In any case, she likes the mother's boyfriend, whom she has been trained to call Uncle. He is her favorite of all of the mother's boyfriends she calls Uncle, and she is willing to believe anything of him.)

Back to the teacher and the question now, yes?

Yes.

The girl sometimes has trouble paying attention, but this happened at a time before kids started coming down with ADHD the way they used to come down with colds and flus. The girl goes undiagnosed, undrugged, and is merely scolded by parents and teachers to pay better attention.

See what I mean?

The girl decides that the truth is to be used only as a last resort. She says, "No, Mrs. Greenberg. I didn't push Colleen down the stairs."

"I have a perfectly good set of eyes," the teacher says. "I saw you do it."

"Okay," the girl says. Though she is willing to lie, she is equally willing to capitulate. It all depends on her mood and where it takes her.

"Okay?" the teacher says. "Is that all?"

"Okay, I pushed her," the girl says. "It was an accident." The two of them are still standing in the schoolyard, where kids loiter and teachers look out of place. There are games of jump rope, skelly, freeze tag, and double Dutch going on. The girl watches kids run and then stop as if paralyzed. One boy is tagged in midstride. He freezes with one arm pumped outward, teetering with one foot raised, waiting for someone to unfreeze him. The girl imagines herself joining in unannounced, heroically tagging the boy to unfreeze him, saving him from the clutches of a frozen life. By now, she truly believes that pushing Colleen was accidental. The girl lives by her whims.

"I don't believe you," the teacher says. "Follow me."

She follows the teacher back to their classroom on the fourth floor. The teacher mumbles as she unlocks the classroom door and turns on the lights. The chalkboards are clean. For the last half hour, kids begged for the chance to wash the boards. The girl has done this before, but only once. She remembers the privileged feeling of standing at the front of the classroom with a basin of warm water and a thick porous sponge at her disposal. First, she erased the boards, wiping away the day's spelling words, math problems, and penmanship lessons in the teacher's looping cursive. Then she dipped the sponge and squeezed it out. Starting at the top of the board, she'd pressed it against the hard slate and dragged it downward, the grayish green chalkboard turning gleaming, wet, black. After several vertical strokes took her to the edge of the board, she'd looked back and seen the board drying in streaks, swaths of water quickly evaporating as if she'd never been there at all.

The teacher waves her over, and even though the girl expects to be struck, she comes. These are the days when everyone has a pass to beat up kids—teachers and neighbors alike—the days when parents thank you for doing it and then bring their kids home and tear them up some more. The girl has seen the teacher yank a boy by the ear to push him into the corner. The teacher points to the nearest seat and says to the girl, "You will sit here for the next hour to think over what you have done. Open your composition book to a fresh page and record your reflections."

"What does that mean?" the girl asks. She is thinking of reflection like in the mirror and, anyway, the teacher lost her once she said the girl had to stay a whole hour. She is supposed to go straight home after school and wait in the apartment until her mother and sister get there. Although she usually lollygags playing in the schoolyard and buying candy in the bodega, she has never gone home an entire hour late.

"I want you to explain why you constantly pick on Colleen. You're nothing but a bully. Perhaps if you can see that in black and white, you'll stop tormenting the poor girl." The girl does not think of herself as mean or as a bully. She doesn't even dislike Colleen. It is just what they do. The girl doesn't think Colleen minds as much as Mrs. Greenberg seems to.

The teacher looks at her watch and slides out of her coat. "Since I am giving you an hour of my unpaid time, you had better make it good."

The pressure. The pressure. The girl has never been good at language arts. She prefers science and the solidity of the earth as she has come to know it; she can stare at the cutaways of the earth, revealing core, mantle, and crust for hours. When she finishes her workbook assignments before the allotted time runs out, she draws volcanoes, paying close attention to her rendering of ash clouds and magma chambers. She doesn't know what Mrs. Greenberg wants her to say, but she opens her notebook to a fresh page. Staring at the chalkboard, which looks lonely with no student, no teacher, no dust, and no words, the girl thinks that if she could write her thoughts all across it, she might be able to produce something beautiful.

The teacher hangs her coat on the back of her adult-sized chair, and the girl realizes that she is still wearing hers. She slips her arms out of the sleeves and drapes it over her shoulders, wearing it like a cape, like She-Ra, Princess of Power. Mrs. Greenberg carries her lesson plan to the boards at the front of the room (the ones at the back are covered with construction paper) and begins copying the next day's spelling words on the far left board. The girl thinks about copying the words now and getting a head start. When all the kids are present, Mrs. Greenberg has to leave the assignments up on each board until every kid has copied them, which can take a while because the kids have to be called up in shifts, the ones from the back rows and the ones with poor eyesight coming forward and crouching with their notebooks balanced on their knees as they get as close to the board as possible. Last year, the girl had twenty-eight classmates. This year, she has forty-four. Pretending to write what Mrs. Greenberg wants, the girl jots down the spelling words. The third word down is *cower*, the fifth word is *intimidate*. The girl stops copying when she realizes that the teacher is trying to make a point.

When Mrs. Greenberg writes at the chalkboard, it is easy to see just how poorly her clothes fit. The girl can see the extra material at the back of her suit jacket billowing out over her waist. The girl's sister works for a company that pays next to nothing, but her clothes fit better than the teacher's. Mrs. Greenberg's shoulder pads are not at the shoulders; they hang down over her biceps. The teacher's sleeves are too long. When her arms are down by her sides, her thumbs disappear, the cuffs swallowing them. The girl is feeling charitable, and so she decides that although the teacher is definitely to blame for her invisible thumbs, she should not be held responsible for the shoulder part. Anyone can see Mrs. Greenberg has weak shoulders.

The teacher's pantyhose are the old-fashioned kind, the kind with the little lines down the back of them, the kind the white women in those old black-and-white movies wear with the skirt suits whose hems fall way past their knees. The seams at the back of the teacher's pantyhose do not follow down her leg in a straight line. They curve around her calves, twisting all the way to the front. Mrs. Greenberg is bowlegged. Perhaps, the girl thinks, this is why her stockings are always crooked.

The stockings make her think of the movies Uncle always brings over. Every time he comes over, he brings a big black garbage bag stuffed full of dirty newspaper, and inside the bag there is always a VCR. He takes out the VCR and hooks it up to the big floor model television in the living room, where everyone can watch. He brings popcorn for the stove and puts in tapes of old movies, of films he said were made when he was little. The girl is a sucker for these movies. She likes Rosalind Russell. Maureen O'Hara. Doris Day. She will watch old movies until her eyes are dry. They sit on the plastic-covered couch, he and the girl and the sister and the mother, watching women telling men to put their lips together and blow, having a good time, until the mother crosses her arms and says, "Thought I was the one you came to see."

Mrs. Greenberg speaks over her shoulder. "How are you making out?" she asks.

"I don't know what to write," the girl says.

Mrs. Greenberg turns from the chalkboard, which is half-filled with tomorrow's lessons. "All right," she says. "Try this. How would you feel if the roles were reversed? What if it were you that was always being pushed or shoved or picked on? What if you were always Colleen's target? How would you like it then? What do you get out of torturing an innocent girl? Think about answering at least one of those questions and see if you come up with something to say."

The teacher raises her eyebrows, implying profundity. The girl remains unimpressed. It could never be the other way around. Colleen is not a leading lady. The girl likens her to the brunettes in the old movies, the ones who never get the guy. The girl is thinking of Ruth Hussey in *The Philadelphia Story* and Janice Rule in *Bell, Book, and Candle*. There is always a Katharine Hepburn or a Kim Novak to tempt the Jimmy Stewarts of the world. Colleen is the kind to get attention only by default.

Though she can hardly remember how it all began, the girl's first push truly was accidental. Mrs. Greenberg assembled the class in two rows by the coat closet, boys on the left and girls on the right. Colleen was in front of the girl, Abdul to her left. As they filed out of the classroom and down the hall to the far stairwell, the girl began to lag behind. She had spotted a small reddish stain in the center of Colleen's skirt. It bloomed brightly as if someone had cut her, as if she'd sat on a tube of paint. Entranced by the blooming, spreading stain—it had no edges, it looked like an inkblot, like something the girl's sister had shown her from an old college psychology textbook before she'd dropped out to make money—the girl lifted her feet mechanically, walking with legs made of wood, knowing Colleen knew things that the girl had yet to learn, wondering if she should follow Colleen more closely so that no one else might see (for surely the girl hadn't noticed the stain when they'd first lined up), when, closing the space between them, the girl stepped too close, right on the back of Colleen's LA Gear sneakers, making Colleen stumble and collide with the girl in front of her. The girl imagined them as a line of dominoes toppling from the one accidental push, but it did not happen like that. Colleen righted herself quickly, but not quick enough to fool Mrs. Greenberg, who walked alongside the class, keeping close to the middle, a vantage point that allowed her to survey the entire line. She cut her eyes at the girl, saying nothing, chalking it up to clumsiness, to an accident. An accident it had been that first time. After that, it simply felt too good to stop. First, there was the closeness of Colleen's body when the girl pushed her, stepping close enough to smell the grease against Colleen's scalp. Second, there was the Jean Naté that wafted from Colleen's collar. When the girl stepped against Colleen, she saw Colleen begging her mother for a splash of cologne from the yellow bottle in the hopes that wearing it would make someone finally notice her. Stepping against the back of Colleen's sneakers was stepping into her life, a life the girl guesses to be less complicated than her own. Colleen, the girl thinks, has a father and no unrelated uncles. When she goes home, someone is always waiting.

The hour draws near. For the past ten minutes, the girl and the teacher have been sitting quietly, trying not to look at each other. The teacher begins to straighten up. "Did you find any answers?"

"I think so," the girl says, though her page is still blank. She takes up her number two pencil and presses the lead deep into the paper, attempting to copy the glamour of Mrs. Greenberg's cursive:

Dear Colleen,

I'm sorry I pushed you down the stairs today and all the other times. I would not like it if you did it back to me. I hope you don't do it, because pushing is wrong, and if you do it just because I did it, then we will both be wrong, which will add up to be more like −2 than 0.

She looks over her words, feeling no remorse, yet hoping this is what her teacher wants. She knows that this is not one of those times where the answer will become clear once she grows older, knows some questions are meant to go unanswered. Like why she has so many uncles if her mother is an only child. Like why Uncle cannot live with them. Or at least leave his VCR.

"If you have any last thoughts, you have five minutes to get them down," the teacher says.

What it really comes down to is the rightness of the push.

When they are going down the stairs and the girl pushes Colleen down the steps or forces her into the railing, the girl feels a part of something larger than herself. She believes, deep down, that Colleen expects it, in fact cannot live without it. On the rare occasions when the girl has not indulged in a minor act of violence, she has caught Colleen sneaking wounded glances at her. Though Mrs. Greenberg can never understand it, the girl knows that Colleen also lives for the skirmish. There were forty-five kids in Mrs. Greenberg's class. If it were not for the girl's attentive violence, Colleen would be a nobody. She'd go unnoticed and uncalled on by Mrs. Greenberg, lost in a sea of indistinguishable black kids in a public elementary school with an overcrowding problem. The girl draws a line through her apology and turns to a fresh page.

Dear Colleen,
You don't have to thank me.

boogiemen

Our mother's voice—raised in anger—followed by the crash of
something sharp, delicate, and expensive shattering against the wall
that was ours on one side and our parents' on the other woke us
up. Dressed in a black full-length slip with pink rollers in her hair,
our mother stood tough by her side of the bed—tough despite the
defeat that sat in her eyes and the tears that rolled down her puffy
cheeks—holding up a picture frame, the muscles on her brown arms
flexed with the need to throw. The picture was barely recognizable
under the layers of dust that had piled up on the cheap frame, but I
knew that it was the picture of us taken at Coney Island two summers
ago. Our father looked relaxed in it. For once, the wary slant of his
mouth had given way to a hesitant smile. Our mother stood on the
opposite end, her hair curled in a flip, her face beaming, looking
like a taller version of Coretta Scott King. My older brother, Julian,
and I stood between the two of them. Julian's eyes were closed; he'd
gotten caught blinking. I had a scowl on my face because I couldn't

have a second candied apple. They took that picture back when we did things as a family, when we went to Coney Island and Mets games during the summer and to the skating rink in Restoration Plaza during the winter. Before my father started spending nights elsewhere, before Julian and I found out that we had a little brother or sister—we never learned which—out in Jamaica, Queens. Before we fell apart.

"Stop it, Anna," our father said as he turned his back to her and continued to pack.

Our mother ignored him. "You see this?" she asked, shaking the frame. "This is a family. Why don't you take this with you to remind you of what you're throwing away?" She made as if to hand it to him. When he reached out to take it, she pulled back. "Or why don't you just throw it away like you're doing to us, Walter? Here, I'll do it for you!" She hurled it against the wall. The dusty glass splintered on impact and the cheap ceramic frame broke off into chunks.

She yelled, "Go on then. Leave! That's what you do best! How these boys gonna eat? Who they gonna look up to with you gone, Walter? Who gonna teach them to become men. Me?"

Our father went over to her, taking deliberately slow steps, and grabbed her by her wrists. He held them both in one of his large hands. "Now you're gonna stop throwing things! You already broke two frames. This how you want the boys to see you?" he asked. She looked over to where we huddled in the corner by the door, gripping each other's hands. Our mother turned to us as if she'd never before seen us in her entire life. Like we were ghosts. It took her a few seconds to focus on our faces. Julian squeezed my hand. A shiver passed from him to me. I squeezed back. Then she smiled and waved us off, "Go back to bed, boys. Everything's all right. Go back to your room and go to sleep."

We beat it back to our room but left the door open so we could hear.

The fights were nothing new. They had been going on for the last two years, ever since we moved from our brownstone in Bed-Stuy to these projects in East New York. We could always hear them arguing, but our mother's anger had always been long-suffering, quiet, and plaintive. It seemed to me that not only had the fights become more frequent but that they had reversed so that they were now more dispassionate on our father's part and more violent on our mother's.

"Think he leaving, Ju?" I asked my brother.

Julian shrugged and climbed onto the top bunk. "He been leaving for two years and ain't never left yet."

We were too caught up in ourselves and our tiny world that summer to be affected by our father's departure. Our world consisted of a six-block radius. It encompassed the intermediate school with the free lunch program and Miller Park across the street from it, the bodegas on Bradford Avenue, the row on Pitkin Avenue, which included the candy store, take-out Chinese, video rental, discount store, and stores that were fronts for people playing the numbers, and a smaller row on Van Siclen Avenue with the pizza shop, liquor store, and dry cleaners. Across from the three main streets were our three blocks of Fiorello projects, which we called first, second, and third. Our projects were stubby, only going up to the fourth floor. There were four projects per block. We lived on Miller between Pitkin and Glenmore.

We were young that summer that our father left us. Julian was almost twelve and I was nine and a half. The weekend after their last fight, we were in our usual spot, seated directly in front of the TV, watching Saturday morning cartoons when our mother called to us.

She came when we didn't answer. "Come with me," she said, standing in front of the TV. She was wearing a cotton dress that hung off her. Our mother had been a good-looking woman, but in less than a week, she became a skeleton of her former self. She seemed slighter, her smooth brown skin now splotchy. Overnight, she seemed to have aged. Lately, the corners of her mouth were always drifting downward.

"Get up!" she said sharply, pulling us up from the floor by the scruffs of our necks as if we were kittens. She took us into her bedroom. With grim determination, she opened Dad's side of the dresser and the left side of the closet so that we could see that all of his stuff was gone. She lifted the edge of the dust ruffle from where it hung to the floor and forced us to peek under the bed. No brightly polished loafers peered back. Our father was truly gone. All of our father's toiletries that usually lined the left-hand side of the dresser were gone. Small circles of clean wood where the toiletries had sat stood out among the dusty, watermarked surface.

"I'm not gonna say this but once, boys. Your father is gone," she said. She released our napes and turned us so that we were face to face.

"Now, I want you to take a good look at each other," she said, her voice a command. So we did.

Julian looked like a miniature version of our father with his high forehead, wary eyes, serious mouth, and stubborn chin. His peasy hair was uncombed, sleep rimmed the corners of his eyes, and his mouth hung slack. His elbows and knees were white with ash and his bony arms were dwarfed by the huge Spiderman T-shirt he'd slept in. The shirt didn't cover his knees—like little knobs they poked out and made his bony giraffelike legs more pronounced. I rubbed my eyes and we stared at each other, unable to comprehend our mother's strange request. Julian looked at me and wriggled his finger near the side of his nostril, pretending to dig in his nose. Grinning, he reached toward me as if to wipe the imaginary booger on my Transformers shirt. I jumped back and our mother grabbed us.

"Stop that!" she said, slapping our arms and clamping down our wrists with a viselike grip. "Be serious now. I want the two of you to understand what I mean. Julian, you take a look at Joseph. Joe, you take a good look at Julian. I mean it!" she snapped.

So we stopped fidgeting and looked again. I looked Julian dead in the eyes and he looked right back at me. It was as if we were playing chicken with our eyes. Neither of us dared to be the first to look away. Looking this time, I didn't see the imaginary booger or the Spiderman T-shirt. I saw the boy who gave me first pick of books at the public library when we went on Fridays to get our books for summer reading. He was my partner for watching the late late shows and all the horror flicks. In my eyes, he was the someone who always had an extra quarter so that I could buy a bag of barbecue potato chips after I had spent all my money on cheap fireworks and water guns that leaked. I saw my brother.

"Now," Ma said. "What do you see?"

Julian looked at me like I was one of those jigsaw puzzles he and our father could spend hours on, slapping me away anytime I tried to point to where a certain piece should go. My face tingled under his inspection.

"I see Joseph. I see my brother," he said solemnly. Then he began to chew on his lower lip. My mother nodded and waited for me.

"I see my brother, Julian," I said and shrugged.

"That's right," she said. "You're the two men of the house now that your dad is gone. You're brothers—blood—and you're all each of you has in this world."

She squeezed tightly on both of our arms and said, "Don't ever forget that." There was an urgency in her voice and her grip that we couldn't understand. It seemed so important to her that we answered and said the right thing. I couldn't know that she was preparing us for the hard times to come, that she was trying to both protect us and make us immune to the things beyond our apartment that would strive to pull us apart.

They began to whisper things about my brother right before school let out that summer. It suddenly became a big deal that Julian had never had a girlfriend when Sasha, a girl in Julian's grade, spread the word that he didn't like girls. Older boys picked on us whenever they saw us around, calling my brother Julie and calling me Josephine. Boys my age that I had previously run around with suddenly wanted to know if I had cooties and if I had caught them from my older brother. No one would let me tag them or borrow their skelly caps and no one would ride the handlebars of my bike. By the end of the summer, I knew that the whispers were fears and confirmations that Julian was what the boys at school called "funny," what my mother called "nasty" and what the adults referred to as "that way."

I was too young to understand the various modes of defense we all set up to safeguard ourselves from looking too closely at my brother. I knew only that the kids were shunning him and that their disdain for Julian was trickling down to me. So I turned my back on him, too. That was the summer I began to venture out past our streets and projects, trying to see what was up in the areas close to us. I was an inner-city anthropologist checking out the locals. That summer, I became fascinated with the kids who lived near Livonia Avenue by the three train and with the boys that played in King Park. I was looking for people who didn't know me, who didn't know that Julian was my brother. I looked for ways to avoid him without appearing to do so. Before, I had enjoyed our late-night horror show marathons, but now I threw tantrums on the evenings our mother would go out to midweek service and leave Julian to watch over me. I didn't know what it meant to be *that way*, but I knew that boys who had once eaten paste with me now brushed themselves off and crossed their fingers if they came into contact with me. I didn't know if what Julian had would rub off on me. And I didn't know if it was temporary like the ringworm I had caught once or permanent like our mother's diabetes.

We were in the candy store on Pitkin and Van Siclen, a block from our house, getting Italian ices when a crew of boys from the first projects came in and saw us. None of them had their shirts on. Their nappy heads were beady with water, their scrawny chests slick with it, and their swim trunks were wet all the way through from spending the afternoon running through the fire hydrant on Bradford Avenue. Their swim trunks had no pockets, which meant that they had no money and no reason for being in the candy store. Except for us. I was hoping they weren't there for us.

They were.

Will's face broke into a grin. "Hey, look what we got here," he said. "A couple of girls buying ices. Hey Julie. Hey Josephine."

We kept our backs to him and waited to be served. I could feel the boys moving behind us, forming a semicircle and fanning around us in a crescent moon of brown bodies. I made sure not to step back into their arc.

Derek called out behind us, "Hey Muhammad give me one, too. Put it on my tab. I ain't got no money."

The man behind the counter said, "You never have money and you never get tab here." All the boys laughed.

Malcolm said to Derek, "That's all right. You don't want him to serve you after he just finished with them homos."

"True that," several boys said. Their voices blended into one large chorus so that I could no longer pick out the individual cadences of their voices and think of them singly.

"Hey Muhammad, you might wanna think about that before you do it," one of the voices called out behind us to the Arab man at the counter as he started to scoop cherry ice from a gallon canister.

"Don't do it, man!" said another.

Someone said, "You could be making the biggest mistake of your life."

"Hey Muhammad, don't be giving that homo no ice cream, man," said one of the voices behind us. It sounded like a boy I knew from the third projects named Kyle, but I hadn't seen him come in with the group. I wondered when he had come in. I no longer knew just how many of them there were behind us and I was too scared to look and see.

Another voice said, "Hey Muhammad, you better be careful who you sell to."

And another, "Yeah, you might get a reputation for selling ice cream to homos."

The man behind the counter looked up, unsure of what they were talking about. He was used to all our bullshit, the way we called him Muhammad without bothering to learn his name, the way we asked how many wives he had, and the way we always asked him if there was pork in the ice cream. But something in their voices triggered him off to the underlying seriousness beneath the joke and warning. The joking had stretched to include him. He straightened and relaxed his hold on the metal ice cream scooper. "What are you all talking about? I don't want trouble here. None of you boys' bullshit now!" he said in his thick accent, suggestive of caravans and savannas.

One of the boys shouted, "No, no man! No bullshit."

This time I recognized Will's voice: "Nah. For real. Didn't you know you got two homos in your store?"

"Homos?" the man behind the counter asked, his accent distorting the word until it sounded like *hummus*.

"Homos," Will said, distinctly, perfectly. "Don't get upset, man. That word probably wasn't in your English-Arab dictionary. Homos. *Homos*," he said. He stepped out to the side of the semicircle. I could see him from the corner of my eye. He pushed his rear end out and pointed to it. He made a circle with his right hand and pushed his left index finger back and forth through it at the same time. He made a face, closing his eyes in ecstasy. The boys behind him joined in with a chorus of, "Ooh! Ooh baby!"

"Homos," Will said. "And I don't wanna eat in no establishment that caters to homos."

One boy threw out, "Yeah, unless you gonna give him a double dip!"

Laughter broke out behind us, the guilty forced laughter that erupts in groups where each person has something to hide. They *had* to laugh. Whoever didn't would be next. The man behind the counter had resumed fixing our ices. Yet when the thread of laughter spooled toward him with its implied threat, his left hand—the one that held the scooper—slowed its scraping motion across the top of the hard-packed gelati. He stiffened, lowering his hand until the scooper fell from it.

The man behind the counter's face turned red. His eyes swung to us. "You boys are brothers, no? You buy ices? You have money? You give it to me now!" he said. He had never before demanded payment first.

"Look man, we got your money," Julian said toughly. "Just like we always do. Now you give us our ices and then you get your money."

"Let me see the money. I don't want no games," he said, his eyes sliding back and forth between us and the boys who circled us.

Maybe Julian realized the futility of fighting. The longer it took for him to give us our ices, the more boys passing by saw the commotion and crowded in behind us. There were already too many of them to count now.

Julian turned to me. "Give him the money, Joe."

"Yeah Josephine, let's see the money," someone said.

"Give him the money, Joe," Julian urged.

"It better not be no Monopoly money," said another.

"Just show it to him! Give him the damn money," Julian said, teeth clenched.

Will shouted, "Show him the money!"

Then they all picked it up. "Show him the money! Show *him* the money! Show him the *mo-ney!*" they chanted behind us as they jostled each other.

"Show him the money! Show *him* the money! Show him the *mo-ney!*" The chant became louder and louder as they closed in the half-circle behind us and got closer and closer.

"Show him the money! Show *him* the money! Show him the *mo-ney!*" They sang tirelessly as if they would never stop. Their voices, jeering, slurring, rang out behind us, louder and closer until their voices seemed to be directly in my ears.

"Show him the money! Show *him* the money! Show him the *mo-ney!*" An arm brushed the back of my hand, a knee slid past my leg. I couldn't step back for fear of them. They were closer than close.

Then Will broke the chant. "Are you sure you wanna take his money, Muhammad? I mean, you don't know where they hands been."

They stopped chanting when Julian screamed, "Joe! Just give him the money!" Julian's voice had risen to a high-pitched strain. His cry, intended to be heard over their chanting, rang out in the stillness. Julian's cry hung in the air between us, disproportionately loud, separate, afraid. His voice seemed about to break. I imagined his vocal cords being stretched out like those exercise rubber bands, about to pop and snap. I had forgotten about Julian there by my side, so lost in the voices singing to me. His brown eyes were wide, frenzied, wild. I could see the whites of them.

They heard Julian's desperation and fed on it. They changed their chant. "*Give* him the money! Give him the money! Give it to him!" they sang, closer and closer.

"Just give it to him or hand it over to me," he whispered. "Please." He stuck his hand out at me. I studied his palm. It had a short life line. It was callused over from playing too much basketball. I couldn't put the money in it. Those boys were behind me, close close close. I could smell them now. The funk of their triumph mixed in with the smell of sweaty skin cooled over by the hydrant's water that clung to their bony arms and chests, rolling down their ashy legs in small beads, collecting in the bottom of their sneakers, making that clucking, squeaking sound as their heels met the squishy insteps of their sneakers and clung to them, rubbing and giving off that faintly sick aroma of dampness, sweaty socks, and rubber. That smell was up my nose and down my throat, becoming part of me. I squeezed my fist on the dollar I was holding. The dollar in my hand was sweating. It burned my palm. I couldn't give it to Julian. I couldn't hand it to the man behind the counter. I couldn't move at all. I was stuck there with the voices, with the smell, with the song and chant, with the closeness that trapped me. I felt the weight of all their eyes on me, boring into my back, heavy enough to snap my neck.

I had to get out.

I threw the crumpled bill on the floor and ran through the crowd of boys, all who quickly backed away so that they wouldn't have to touch me. I ran out the store and down the street, leaving my brother behind.

I ran until my chest began to burn. When I stopped I was down by where the J and Z trains ran above the streets down Atlantic Avenue. I vaguely knew that Maxwell's Bakery was near in one direction and that the McDonald's was not far in the other, but none of the streets themselves looked familiar. I had come to a place outside of my neighborhood. I was where no one knew me as Julian's brother or knew that he was *that way*. I thought of that moment in the store and felt all of my anger at Julian return. Anger at my brother and fear of the thing that he was and hurt that he had not pulled me to the side and told me but made me find out from everyone else—all of these feelings filled me as I slowly made my way back home, kicking every can or bottle in the street that I could find. I hated him for what he had done to me. He'd made me think that we were blood brothers, that we were close, like two heartbeats beating in tandem. But it was a lie. How could we be when he was what he was?

"Where's your brother?" my mother asked when I finally slunk back into the house. Her back was turned to me as she washed dishes in the sink.

"I don't know. I don't care. Probably out there sucking somebody's dick, that nasty ass homo."

"What?" she asked, turning to me with quicksilver speed. "What did you just say, Joseph?" she asked me, carefully, neutrally. I could have heard the slyness in her voice if I had chosen to listen, but I began to repeat what I had just said without thinking when her heavy hand came out of nowhere and caught me across my mouth. The tiny diamond of her engagement ring nicked my cheek from the force of the blow. I staggered back, feeling the burn and sting of the air making contact with the fresh blood that rose to the surface of my cheek.

"You not too old to be beat, you know." She grabbed me by my arm and pulled me back to her. I knew what was coming next, but I couldn't believe that she would dare. She dragged my struggling body over to the kitchen table and managed to pull out a seat for herself. "Let me go! Get off me!" I said, kicking my feet out to loosen her hold on me.

Her voice was deadly calm when she said, "You had better be still."

She sat down and pulled me on top of her lap. I knew better than to talk back or even act like I was trying to resist, but I wasn't about to be humiliated by a beating. "Let me go! I ain't do nothing!" I said, squirming once again.

"Oh yes you did! Don't never let me catch you saying something dirty like that again! Take your belt off and hand it to me."

"No."

My mother cocked her head to one side and appraised me, looking me over. "Oh really? So you wanna make this more difficult than it needs to be, huh?" she said as she held me down. She slid my belt through its loops with a vengeance and yanked it free so that she could beat me with my own belt. She nudged my shorts and briefs down. A shock of cool air hit my buttocks and I squirmed harder. Until I got the first taste of the belt. It sliced through the air and hit my naked skin so hard my whole body leaped up. Her hand pressed down hard into the center of my back to keep me still. "I didn't raise you to talk filth and I don't wanna hear no mess like that never again! You know what you said is wrong. Why you say something like that? About your own brother?" my mother said, in between whacks from the belt. Her voice was louder and harder than the sound of new leather on nine-year-old skin.

"I can say whatever I want. It's true!" I screamed.

"It's not true!" she yelled back.

"Sasha said so! Everybody said so! It's true. Everybody knows," I said, my voice rising higher as my face began to overheat. I knew what was coming, but I couldn't stop it. And I hadn't cried since I was a little kid.

"I don't give a damn who said what and who saw what!" She ignored my evidence and whacked me again. "They lyin'!" she said, her voice reaching a feverish pitch and telling me what she needed to believe was true.

But I kept on, "And now they say it everywhere we go! Everything he does means something now. And me, too! They say me, too! And Julian . . . he won't do or say nothing! He just stand there and let them say—" Then it came. I couldn't stop it. I started to cry as I told her what happened in the store. The hot tears that I hadn't cried when my mother told me my father was gone, tears that wouldn't come when we went to Grammy's funeral last Easter, tears that knew better than to appear whenever I fell off my bike and ripped my skin open or burned my fingers with firecrackers, those tears now all came in a rush, falling on my mother's lap in dark little spots that spread and dampened and darkened the material of her dress, squeezing out from a tight knot in the center of my chest, pushing up through my ribs, crowding my throat, threatening to choke me if I couldn't cry them fast enough, forcing me to gulp some back in order to breathe.

"So you *left* him there?" she said and whipped me harder. "I don't believe you! Sitting here crying and caterwauling about how *you* feel. He's the one they was picking on! How you think *he* feel, knowing his own brother ain't got his back?" she said. Then she laid the belt gently across the backs of my legs and gave me two sharp stinging slaps with her hand, "*This* is for talking back and *this* is for not listening to me when I tell you to do something. Now get up and fix your clothes."

Her eyes were dead when she looked at me. She said, "I don't know how you could be my son. You must be your father's son. Just run when things get a little tough. Too scared to fight it out, too caught up in your own self to see somebody else through."

"You the one told us not to play nasty," I said, reminded of the beatings we'd get when girls ran home and said we'd tried to play doctor with them or when we were outside with the rest of the boys trying to see who could pee the farthest.

"But I also told you that you and your brother got to cling to each other 'cause you all each other got, Joseph. I don't care if Julian run up and down Pitkin Avenue naked for nothing except a cow bell. I might not like it or approve, but I don't abandon him. 'Cause he's my son. My life's blood. And he's your blood. You don't never turn your back on your brother. On your blood. No matter what. You hear me?"

"Yes, ma'am," I said, drying my eyes with the backs of my hands.

"Good. Now get out my face," she said and handed me back my belt. I knew better than to snatch it. I took it carefully and walked stiffly to my room and threw myself face down across the bottom bunk. I heard the sucking sound of water down the drain and knew she had unstopped the sink.

"And you can finish these dishes before I get back," she said. I didn't ask her where she was going and she didn't volunteer any information. I heard the slam of our door and the three locks being snapped into place.

The sky turned dark long before they returned home.

I was waiting up for them in front of the living room TV, watching the late late show when I heard the key in the lock.

My mother didn't say a word. After she checked first in the sink to make sure I had done the dishes, she marched Julian to the kitchen and heated up the leftovers from dinner for him. As she put a glass of juice and a plate of food in front of Julian, she shot a look over his head at me. That look was a warning and a reminder, both an encouragement to go talk to my brother and a threat of another beating if I didn't. When I got up from my place on the floor and made my way into the kitchen, she walked away and left us alone.

"Hey," I said as I sat down at the table with him. He looked long at me with wounded eyes, pleading for me to say more. These were the eyes that had scrutinized me that night Mama made us look so carefully at each other. I wondered what he had seen that night and if it had prepared him for a night like this. Either I had not looked closely at Julian or I had not looked long enough because I had not seen this, this thing that would separate us and divide us, that would breed ignorance, bravado, and fear. I had only looked to see myself in his eyes. I had looked at him to see my future, my face in a few years, what I would become. I had not seen him at all. Now that I could see, I had no words to take it back. We stared at each other for what seemed like hours. Again, neither of us wanted to be the first to look away. Finally, Julian turned his back on me, cutting me with firm dismissal. He downed his juice in one gulp and picked up his plate of food and went to our bedroom with it. He slammed the door, and in a minute, his boom box blared and drowned out whatever I could have thought to say.

By the time Julian emerged from his room, I was halfway through *Tales from the Crypt*.

He dropped his dishes in the sink and ran water over them while I pretended to be engrossed in the film. Just when he was about to walk away I leaned closer to the television as if I couldn't take my eyes off of what I was watching. "Oh snap," I said, knowing that Julian would hear me. He tried to see what I was looking at, and when he couldn't see the screen, he came into the living room and leaned himself up against the wall near the light switch. "What you watching?" he said, asking as if he didn't care.

"*Tales from the Crypt*," I said.

"What's this one about?"

"Some boogieman something," I said. To tell the truth, I couldn't even remember what the story was or which kind of creature this one was about. Before I started deserting him that summer, Julian and I used to catch every scary flick that came on. And we never missed *Tales from the Crypt*. When I was younger, before I learned to distinguish between creatures from the black lagoon, werewolves, boogiemen, the living dead, ghouls, and vampires, I called all the monsters boogiemen. The name stuck.

"Where were you for all that time?" I asked.

"Out."

"Why you ain't come back till just now?"

"Didn't feel like it," he said.

"You all right?"

"Yeah."

"Good."

"How is it?" Julian asked, edging closer to the living room, keeping his hands in his pockets.

"It's all right. Nothing special." I stopped breathing. Sitting there with every body part tensed, I was wondering if he had forgiven me.

"Scary?"

"Nah."

"How many people got killed so far?"

"None. Nobody ain't even dead yet."

"That's weak," he said, sitting down on the couch beside me. He took an end of the thin blanket I had spread across me and yanked some more to his side.

"Yeah," I said, letting out my breath.

During a commercial, the sound of our mother's loud breathing came to us from down the hallway, where she had fallen asleep with her bedroom door open, trying to eavesdrop on us and see if we had worked things out. Briefly, before the show came back on, I wondered if she had known or just merely hoped that everything would turn out all right. I decided that it didn't really matter. Then I looked at my brother across from me, wearing the face I would one day inherit, a face that was our mother's and father's and mine and yet, I realized, a face that was also his and his alone. A face I had to respect, even if I could not understand it or read it.

Now we were like always. Sitting on the couch with the thin blanket spread over our knees, ready to throw it over our heads during the scary parts, peeking over the top so that we could see and not see. The film had finally started to get good. The monster was catching people left and right. I was clutching my corner of the blanket in a death grip, tensing when the music sped up, flinching every time I expected the monster to strike a blow. As always, it became so real to me that I felt like it was me running through the woods screaming even though there was no one around for miles to hear. And no one to save me. My heart was in my throat. Then I remembered that my brother was there with me. So I turned to him and whispered, "Ju?"

"Yeah?" Julian peeked out from under the covers, the bottom half of his face lost in the blanket, scared just like me until he saw me looking at him. He dropped the blanket like it was on fire.

"You scared?"

He shook his head, the trace of a smile evident. "Nah," he said. "Ain't nothing to fear."

dance for me

The girls on Lexington had it the worst. Hated maroon skirts the color of dried blood. Navy blazers complete with gaudy emblem. Goldenrod blouses with Peter Pan collars. And knee socks. Actually, knee socks weren't so bad. Knee socks served their purpose in the winter, keeping sturdy calves warm.

The girls on East End wore gray or navy skirts, plain and not pleated, with a white blouse, sweater optional.

Multiple skirts were another way to go. We had our choice of navy, gray, maroon, and an unpleated light blue seersucker meant only for the spring. The choices allowed us to pretend we weren't really wearing a uniform. We hoped merely to be thought eccentric. Girls with a penchant for skirts with panels. But we fooled no one. Our uniforms, our talk, our walk, our avid interest in grooming and normal people's clothing, and our daily preoccupation with what we would wear on upcoming field trips when allowed to be out of uniform filled our time and conversations. We had a special way of standing that was part lean, part slouch, as if posture was too much of a bother to consider.

Nameless, faceless on a school trip, we stood out. Solid-colored blouses, pleated skirts, knee socks, and loafers, bluchers, or oxfords. Private school girls. Not to be confused with Catholic school girls. Or reform school girls (how many times did the kids in my neighborhood look at me in condescending pity?). Not to be confused with the girls from *The Facts of Life*. They were boarders. No matter how many times I tried to explain this, the kids in my neighborhood persisted in calling me Tootie.

We attended a second-tier all-girls school. It wasn't as illustrious as the private schools on the Upper East Side nor as seedy as the ones in Midtown. We clung to our small but unique differences. For example, having our choices of uniforms made us the envy of the other all-girls schools. Girls were sure to take it out on us during soccer games. Secondly, there was our partnership with a nearby all-boys school, our "brother" school two blocks away, which allowed us to have kissing partners whenever we put on a play.

At school, there were the WASPS and the JAPS. And me. Girls with last names for first names. Riley. Taylor. Haley. Morgan. Hayden. Girls whose names are meant for a boy or girl, depending.

I'd never told anyone this, but I always felt naked in my pleated skirt, vulnerable. There was a trick to rolling the skirt that would take several inches off, a way of folding tightly and minutely that would allow one to hide the extra material beneath a shirt if tucked then pulled out just enough to camouflage the extra bulk. Only I didn't know it. I'd seen it numerous times, jealously watching girls enter the bathroom with skirts that covered their knees and walk back out with skirts that skimmed their thighs, but I still couldn't get it. The lines of my pleat were never quite right, always drooping in the front, making me look slightly off kilter.

It was lunchtime and I was in the school's bathroom with my stomach bared to the mirror as I tried to roll my skirt when Taylor and

Ashley entered and headed for the stalls, deep in conversation. Neither of them noticed me.

"Well, I wouldn't go with a guy from Buckley, that's for sure."

"I might not get to go at all. We're supposed to go to the Hamptons and my dad really has his heart set on it. How am I supposed to get out of it?"

"I don't know. I so need a new pair of jeans. Do you want to go to the Gap today after we get out of chorus?"

"Um, yeah. Hey, did you hear Heather's parents let Chase go to Cabo San Lucas with her for spring break?"

"No."

"They even paid his way."

So caught up in eavesdropping on their conversation, I didn't hear the squeal of the bathroom door the second time it opened. Heather walked in alone and went straight to the mirror. She frowned slightly when she heard herself being discussed. Then she went into a stall near theirs.

"Who said that?"

"Heather, that's who."

"I heard she broke up with him."

"For the coxswain? That's like way over."

"What happened?"

"He dumped her for a girl from Chapin."

Two toilets flushed simultaneously. By the time Taylor and Ashley emerged, I'd whipped out my Carmex and pretended to be carefully moisturizing, all thoughts of fixing my skirt gone. They washed their hands and walked out without looking at me.

Once they left, Heather came out of her stall.

Moments like these were common. They happened several times during the day—self-reflective moments where girls met in between classes, gathering in bathrooms and on stairways to consider the grave issues of the times and their place in the world. Usually the person being discussed wasn't present.

Heather was still standing there. Her eyes met mine in the mirror. "It's not true, you know."

"What?"

"I never went out with that guy. Never even kissed him. He was a total turd."

I shrugged. "Okay."

She scrutinized me. "You're in my class."

I nodded. "Yeah."

"Do you know about the party on West Ninety-first this Friday?"

"At Trinity?"

"Are you going?"

I pretended to give the question some thought. The parties were hosted by coed private day schools who issued invitations to certain schools, who then issued memberships to certain students. She knew I couldn't go. The memberships were a subtle way of excluding the undesirables. The membership lists went out in sixth grade. The scholarship girls who came in through the enrichment programs started in seventh grade. There was no way ever to be included on the lists, unless someone sponsored me, which no one ever did. I had no plans to go to the party this Friday or any other Friday and she knew it.

"I wasn't planning on it," I said.

"Oh. Do you know how to do that new dance they're doing?" she asked me. "You know the one that goes like this." Heather's gyrations resembled nothing I could identify.

"Um no, I can't say that I know that one," I said. "Sorry."

"Maybe I'm doing it wrong," she said.

"Maybe."

"It's called running something."

"The running man?"

"That's it!" She touched my arm. "Do you know it?"

"Sure."

"Can you show me?"

I looked around. "Here? In the bathroom?"

"Yeah." Heather smiled at me, warm and eager. I really didn't want to. I wasn't a very good dancer and I didn't like to perform. At home, I would sing only in the shower, and I danced at house parties only when the lights were very low. But I danced for her, awkward at first, since there was no music, but she didn't seem to notice or mind. Once I started dancing, her eyes never met mine. They were riveted instead to my legs and feet. I had a feeling she wanted to take notes.

"That looks so hard," she said.

"It's not," I huffed. I danced harder, wanting to show off. I was silently repeating the words of a popular song in my head to give myself a beat. I danced harder as I tried to incorporate moves I'd seen on *Video Music Box*, getting ahead of myself and quickly losing the beat. A video diva I had never been, watching videos only on Saturdays when my mother was out. I was losing my rhythm and running out of breath when she finally said, "Wow. You're good. Really, really good."

I stopped and took a deep breath. I smiled. "Thanks."

That evening, our phone rang, something it hardly ever did. My mother eyed the phone suspiciously, letting it ring three times before picking up. "Hello?" she answered warily, frowning at the unseen offender who'd interrupted her silence.

"Yes, hold on." She held the phone out to me. "It's for you?" I ignored the question in her voice and grabbed it.

"Hi, it's me."

"Hi. It's Heather," she said, as if I wouldn't know her voice.

"Hey."

Who is it? my mother mouthed silently.

Heather, I mouthed back. *From school.*

It had been my mother's idea to put me in the enrichment program that had given me a scholarship for the all-girl's school, a decision she'd come to regret in the face of my loneliness and unpopularity. Now, she hovered and tried to listen in, filled with hope.

Heather's excitement came through, giddy and loud. "You're coming! You are so coming," she shrieked into my ear.

"What are you talking about?"

"The party this Friday. Did you forget?"

"No, I remember."

"Well, I got you in. I sponsored you," she said. There was a pause in her voice, as if she was waiting for something.

"Thanks," I said.

"You don't sound excited."

"I am."

"You are going to go, right?"

I didn't answer. I was taking my time to think about it. Although she'd sponsored me, there was still the question of clothing. I had nothing suitable to wear. The dance would also end late and I didn't think my mother would want me riding home from Manhattan to Brooklyn that late at night by myself. "Well—"

"Nadira is going," Heather said, as if it made a difference.

Nadira was the other black girl in our class. She'd been at the school since kindergarten. There were a number of affluent black and Asian girls in my school, and we claimed no kinship with one another. If I closed my eyes and listened to them speak, I wouldn't know they weren't white. Though Nadira and I belonged to the same race, she had more in common with the white girls. She and they lived in the same neighborhoods, had the same friends, values, and ideals. They listened to z100 and sang classical in the choir. Like the white girls, she could not dance. I couldn't either, but no one knew that. They all took it for granted that I could.

"I'd like to, but I don't think my mom will let me because it ends so late."

"Tell her that's no problem. I wanted you to stay over. I'm having a little get-together at my house after the dance. You know, an after-the-party party. Just a couple of girls. A sleepover. Taylor. Maya. Ashley and maybe some others. Ask your mom if it's okay."

I held the receiver to my chest. "Mom? Heather wants to know if it's okay if I sleep over at her house this Friday." Heather lived in a penthouse on Ninety-fifth and Park. Of course it was okay.

Heather invited me to sit with her at lunch the next day. Four girls smiled at me as I sat, and then they continued on with their discussions.

"I have this body suit and I'm going to wear it with my white jeans," Maya said. The other girls nodded their approval.

"You should wear your hair half up and half down," Heather told her.

"I don't have anything to wear. I'm going to need something new," Taylor said.

"Let's go to the Gap after class today and find something," Ashley suggested.

They were all wearing fleeced pullovers in different colors from L.L. Bean or Patagonia over their collared blouses and they were wearing heather gray leggings beneath their pleated skirts. None of them had on socks. Their feet were bare in their loafers, docksiders, and bluchers.

I excused myself to go to the bathroom. There, I peeled off my socks. Ashley followed behind me. When I stood up, socks in hand, she said, "Um, do you think you could show me the dance you showed Heather?"

The next day, I was back in the bathroom, showing five new girls. For the next two days, Heather brought girls to me and we took them into the bathroom to teach them the steps. For the next two days, I danced and danced on the cold white tiles while white girls leaned against sinks and stall doors and watched. The dancing, I thought, brought me respect and admiration. Through it, I was redeeming myself in their eyes. I was, after all these years, good for something.

The day before the dance, Heather caught me on my way out to the train station. "I've been meaning to tell you this. About the party on Friday." Hands jammed into her jacket pockets, she stood on one foot, the other snaked around her calf, rubbing the back of her leg with the toe of her shoe.

My stomach tightened. Now she'd tell me it had all been a joke. They'd been teasing me. Making me feel as though I fit in was a prank some upperclasswoman had put them up to. "What about it?"

"Well, I know I told you there were just going to be girls at the party, but I wanted to make sure you'd come. There are going to be a few guys there, too. Don't worry, they're cool. They're guys I know from St. Bernard's, Allen-Stevenson, Buckley, and Collegiate."

"But—"

"They're going to sleep in the den. We'll meet them at the party and they'll come back with us. Is that cool?"

"Yeah," I said, relieved that her groundbreaking news had nothing to do with me.

"Good. Look, the girls and I chipped in on this. We were wondering if you could score us some weed? We want to have some real fun. I hope this is enough," Heather said, pressing crinkly bills into my hand. She patted my arm and stepped off the curb to hail a cab to take her home. I clutched the money in my hand, walked down Lexington to catch the four train, and rode home.

When I got home that night, I searched in my mother's sewing basket until I found her seam ripper. I removed the deadly thing and carefully pulled off the stitches surrounding the little horse on the back pocket of my jeans.

I changed into these jeans, a trial run for the real test tomorrow. I was surprised to see myself in regular clothes. I changed shirts and threw on a light jacket. I counted out the money Heather had given me, folded it neatly, and slipped it into my pocket.

"Where are you going?" my mother asked when she saw me at the door.

"Out."

She didn't ask for any further explanation. Something had changed between us ever since the phone call. My blossoming friendships pleased her. My mother was as happy as if the invitation had been extended to her. Just yesterday, she'd put her hand on my shoulder while I was washing dishes. "I just want you to be happy," she'd said, her guilt now assuaged.

There was a store two blocks away that I knew was just a front. I'd gone in once to buy snacks and everything they sold me was expired, stale. I pushed through the door and walked in. One teenager hunched over an arcade game and two lounged against the corners of the wall. Twenty-five-cent bags of popcorn, potato chips, and cheese curls, ten-cent lollipops, and five-cent Peanut Chews and pieces of Super Bubble were behind a counter covered in Plexiglas.

I walked up to the counter.

"Can I buy some weed here?"

I could feel everyone look at me. The man behind the counter squinted. He cleared his throat. He took a long time before he spoke. "We got soda and chips. What you see, that's what we got."

"But I want to buy some weed," I said. "I have money."

"We sell candy, soda, and chips," he said. "You wanna buy some candy?"

I didn't know what else do to. I was frustrated, wanting to argue.

He knew it was a weed spot; I knew it was a weed spot. Was there some magic word I needed to say, some secret code that would let him know I meant business?

I pulled my money out and held it up to the Plexiglas. "Open sesame," I said.

He shook his head. I walked out.

A minute later, I felt someone behind me. I turned. I recognized him from the store; he'd been playing Pac-Man. "What was you doing in there? You crazy or something?"

I walked faster. "Leave me alone."

"That was real stupid. What, you not from around here?"

"I live here," I told him.

He didn't believe me. "Where?"

"Miller and Pitkin."

"I live on that block and I never seen you."

"Well, I go to school," I said.

His lips curled up then. They were full, made brown from smoking. His eyes were large, round, sleepy. He was older. Beautiful. I felt my mistake. "I didn't mean it like that."

He walked by my side. "So why you wanna buy weed?"

"Just to try it," I said. "For fun."

"You ever smoke a blunt before?"

"I didn't want a blunt. I wanted a joint."

He looked at me like I was stupid. "I was going to buy it for my friends," I said. "They asked me to get it for a party."

"So, you still want it?"

"Five dollars for a nickel bag, right?"

"You been watching too much TV," he said.

He refused to give it to me out on the street.

"Let's take a walk." We walked past my block and past the intermediate school to the park.

He stopped when we got to the swings. He sat down on one and backpedaled with his feet. "Come here."

I stood between his legs; we were eye to eye.

"What's your name?" he asked.

"You don't need to know."

He nodded. "So, you like white boys."

"No," I said.

"Black guys?"

"Nope."

"Girls?" he asked, his voice filled with disbelief and excitement.

"I don't like anybody," I said.

He pulled me toward him and kissed me. The faint sweet scent of smoke clung to his chin and I knew that I would smell of him. I had a feeling as if I were waiting in the subway for my train just before it pulls in and it was rushing down the track, blowing its dirty hot wind underneath my skirt, caressing the bare skin between pleats and socks. I tried to pull away but felt his hands cupping my butt, felt him slip the bag of weed into my back pocket. He turned me away from him, adjusting me so that I sat on his front thighs. Pretending to put his arms around me, he slipped his hands into my front pockets, seeking until he found my folded cash. Slick, I thought. Smooth. To anyone passing by, we looked like two fools making out in the park.

The party, because I had longed for it, was a disappointment. The deejay could not mix one song into another. The lights never got very low. We stood in a papered gymnasium, in jeans, stretchy shirts, and too many coats of mascara. Girls from different schools divided themselves accordingly. Even without their uniforms, I could pick out the girls from Brearley, Chapin, and Spence. The boys Heather knew didn't show up until the end of the party. The only people I really knew were Heather, Taylor, Maya, and Ashley, and every time I saw them, they were all dancing, proudly showing off the moves I'd taught them. I ran into Nadira once that night when we were both getting sodas, but she didn't speak to me. I held up the wall all night. No one asked me to dance. I held my plastic cup of soda and thought of my mother at home, sleeping blissfully, happy and proud.

I had only one chance to talk to Heather at the dance. She came over to where I stood on the wall, her face flushed from dancing. "Did I do okay?" she asked me.

"You look good," I said.

"How do you like it?"

I shrugged. "It's okay."

"Aren't you dancing?"

"Nobody asked me."

"They probably don't want you to embarrass them," Heather said. I didn't bother to tell her that the dance I'd shown her was the only one I knew. "Don't worry," she said. "The real party starts when we get to my house."

At Heather's house, we had carte blanche. Her parents were asleep. Heather brought out the alcohol, I pulled out the small bag of weed, and we wasted no time getting drunk and high. A boy Heather had introduced as Gabe wanted to play a version of spin the bottle.

I was the first victim. Gabe and I looked at each other across the thin neck of the bottle, unsure.

"He's never made it with a black girl before," Taylor said.

"So?"

"Go in the closet with him," Heather suggested. "Show him how it's done." She clapped me on the arm and gave me a push. Gabe held out his hand and I got up, unsteadily, taking it. I wasn't sure that I wanted to go, but I went.

We sat in the deep closet; the hems of Heather's jackets grazed the tops of our heads. I decided I couldn't, wouldn't do it. Gabe slid a finger up my arm and I shivered, backing away. "Wow, this closet is really big, huh?"

"It's cool," he said. "We don't have to, you know, I mean unless you want. . . ." He looked hopeful even in the dark.

"I can't," I said.

"Maybe if you touch it." He took my hand and rubbed it against his denim crotch, his hand over mine.

"I'm going to be sick," I said.

"Whoa, wait a minute," he said. "Okay."

"Sick sick sick," I said.

He leaned back, but in a minute he asked, "Can I touch your breasts?"

"I don't think so."

"Just once?" He reached under my shirt. My bra was lace, one of my mother's cast-offs. My underwear did not match, but I knew he would never know that.

"Hey," he said, feeling the lace cups of my bra. "Whoa. Hey."

"Whoa. Hey," I said, mocking him, feeling suddenly warm.

His hand closed over my breast and squeezed. It made me think of the old-fashioned cars in a Bugs Bunny cartoon. "Beep beep," I said, then burst out laughing.

He laughed, too, and then the two of us couldn't stop laughing. We fell against each other, laughing. Then he pulled me through the jackets and across his lap, pushing his tongue into my mouth, banging his teeth against mine, kissing me wet and sloppy. I tasted the strong flavor of weed on his tongue and thought of the boy who'd sold it to me, how beautiful he'd been, how though we lived just a few blocks apart, we were strangers. Like the boy pressing himself against me; we were from different worlds. They were both from the real world, their own distinct ones, but I was somewhere in limbo. Set apart, I didn't know how to let either of them in.

Gabe's hands were tugging my shirt down, and I knew that in

a minute they'd be working the latch of my bra, but I didn't stop him. In the dark of Heather's closet, I tried to see what Gabe saw. I pictured an image of myself that was Heather's body and face, only it was black and it was me. I saw how much of me would change; I saw the girl I would become. And I decided to go ahead and miss myself right now, knowing that the girl I would become wouldn't know how to appreciate me at all.

girl of wisdom

Fifteen and too shy to do anything on her own, Melanie waits for Chandra to come down. Waits at the large, wide window—the thin curtains Bernice has hung do not cover the width of it—for just a glimpse of Chandra, because Bernice will not let her come over. Will never let her come over. And so she and Chandra must meet here outside on the stoop, in full view of the wide window and the neighborhood, where Bernice can, as she is fond of saying, "keep an eye on things." Bernice is in the kitchen baking, though it is much too hot for that and Melanie hardly ever eats anything. Bernice has the radio going in the kitchen. The music, which Melanie tries to ignore, has her mother moving in time as though she were still young and still slim. It is the Isley Brothers. Or the Whispers. Or some such quartet or quintet of men with outdated hairdos.

Chandra emerges from their building, sunglasses perched on her head, holding a small brown bag and a section of newspaper. "I'm going outside!" Melanie calls, as she steps into her shoes, glad to be away from her mother, who she always calls Bernice, even to her face, just to show that she feels no closeness.

They spread the newspapers out on the hot concrete steps and sit down. Chandra passes the bag of sunflower seeds and Melanie grabs a handful, cracking them open between her teeth and spitting the shells onto the stoop. Chandra waves at a boy across the street, motioning him over. "Watch this," she says.

"You know him?"

"I'm about to," Chandra says. She calls out, "Hey boy! Give me a dollar, and I'll give you something in return!"

Once he gets closer, she wrinkles her nose in disgust. "Phee-eew! Your breath stink so bad I can smell it from across the street!" The two girls laugh at the boy's retreating back.

As they sit, Chandra makes a game of it, teasing the boys, selecting them at random, rewarding some and ridiculing others on a whim. After a while, she turns to Melanie and says, "You next."

"Not me."

"Scared?"

"I just don't like young boys," Melanie says. "They immature."

The boys are the same age as Chandra and Melanie. Melanie is tired of these kinds of boys. Boys that dress in oversized but expensive fashions, boys without a dollar to their names, or as Bernice says, boys "without a pot to piss in or a window to throw it out of."

Music blares from an opened window on the third floor of their building and down into the street. The two girls listen to it and idly watch the traffic slow to a stop at the light. Chandra pushes Melanie, pointing to an old black Oldsmobile three cars behind the light. "That's what you need."

"That old man?"

"You said boys too immature."

"If I give him some, he probably have a heart attack."

"Let's see." Chandra calls out to him, "Hey Pops! My friend says she likes you."

"Stop," Melanie whispers.

The man looks at them, shaking his head in annoyance.

"For real!" Chandra cries.

"Then let her say it herself," the man says, his voice carrying.

Chandra turns to Melanie, waiting.

"I got something you might like," Melanie says, not knowing she is going to say it until it comes out.

"And what's that?" he asks. The light changes and he lets the cars behind him go around.

"I can't show it to you here," she says. "It's private."

"You young girls playing games with me?" he asks.

"Age ain't nothing but a number," Melanie says.

"That's right, you tell him," Chandra encourages.

He parks in front of the hydrant. When he starts to get out of the car, Melanie shrinks back and retreats up her steps. "You better go get you some Viagra first before you think you can handle me, grandpa!"

One week later, Melanie is outside on the stoop, enjoying the early fall weather that still feels like summer, still thinking of the afternoon when she'd teased the old man. Feeling a thrilling rush of pleasure at the thought of him. Days after she had humiliated the man, she found herself thinking of him. More than once, she thought—hoped—she sighted his car. She'd even offered to run errands for Bernice. Taking her mother's clothes to the cleaners, Melanie found herself staring into the faces of the older men she encountered, sure that each one was him, following her, watching her, waiting for a chance to take her away.

Children rush out of the apartment building and Melanie grabs the railing to avoid the swinging door and to steady herself. She looks up at the sound of a horn, sees the black car idling alongside the hydrant.

It is him. The old man from a week ago. She quickly smoothes her denim skirt and crosses her legs at the ankle, partly afraid, partly brimming.

He watches her alertly, almost daring. "Not so brave without your girlfriend? No one around to bolster your courage?" he taunts.

She doesn't like the way he says it even though it is true. When Chandra was with her, she was fearless, not her mother's daughter. She was a different girl, invincible. The kind of girl that expected men to notice her and then acted like she didn't care when they did.

But Chandra isn't with her now and Melanie doesn't need her to be. She shifts on the stoop, parts her legs wide beneath her skirt. "I don't need courage," she says.

The man waits, not getting out of the car.

Melanie rises from the stoop and steps carefully around the sections of dirt and weeds between the cracks of the sidewalk's broken pavement and walks to the man's car.

He pushes the passenger door open. "Get in."

The man doesn't speak for some time after she gets in the car. He doesn't reach over and try to grab her or do anything to make her uncomfortable. He turns the volume down on the stereo; he is listening to an oldies station. Melanie sizes him up on her side. He doesn't look as old up close. He smells of Old Spice, safe and comforting. It was the smell that the men from Bernice's hometown wore when they used to visit. It was the smell that came to Melanie whenever those men crouched to press a dollar into her hand, sending her to play while they sat in the living room with her mother. It was the smell that lingered in the house long after the men stopped coming.

Finally, he asks her, "Do you do this a lot?"

"What?"

"Pick up old men?"

"You the one that came back looking for me," she reminds him.

"I just wanted to see what you would do," he says, looking at her. "I'll drive you back now."

"No."

"What will your mother think about you disappearing?"

"Bernice won't notice."

"Bernice?"

"That's my mother."

"You shouldn't address her so. That's insolence," he says.

He seems angry, but Melanie doesn't know that word so she nods as if she understands, not wanting to disappoint. She doesn't like him talking about disappearing, though. For the first time, since meeting him, her actions seem foolish to her. "Anyway, I'm not disappearing. I'm just hanging out with you for a little while. Then I'm going back home," she says, with more confidence than she feels.

"I should take you home now," the man says, but Melanie knows he won't.

"You smell the way my father used to." She touches the sharp crease in his pants leg.

"How's that?"

Like Old Spice. Like good times. Like Sunday mornings. "Your cologne."

He peels her hand off him. "I'm not your father. I have children older than you. I don't need a daughter. You're a foolish little girl; I'm only interested in women."

"I *am* a woman," she says, though tears fill her eyes.

The man looks at her, unspeaking. He reaches over her, pulls a handkerchief out of his glove compartment, and hands it to her silently. She dabs at her eyes. "Don't cry. You'll sog my whole car with those tears," he says. "You don't know what a woman's tears do to me."

"I don't want to go home yet."

He considers her. "You have a name, girl?"

Melanie stares straight ahead and refuses to speak. She holds her hands out in front of her to count the calcium deposits on her fingernails, imagining one boyfriend for each white splotch.

"My name is Milton. As in *Paradise Lost*."

"What's that?"

"A famous book written by a blind poet."

"If he was so blind, then how did he write it?" Melanie asks, doubting.

"His daughters wrote it down it for him."

Melanie thinks of how Bernice tries to make her do things she doesn't want to and feels sorry for those daughters. She sees them sitting in a dusty parlor. Hovering over papers and desks, scribbling, squinting, and straining in the dim, mote-filled light. She wonders why they didn't write something else instead. Their own stories. Or love letters. Why they had not fooled their father, tricked him, made him pay. If it had been her, she would have at the very least lain his clothes out in the most outrageous combinations and told him that they matched.

He asks, "How old are you?"

On a good day, she thinks she can pass for twenty. "I'm old enough to do whatever I want," she says, reveling in her power.

"And what do you want to do? Nice girls don't get into cars with strangers." She catches him eyeing her again. "Then again, you don't look like such a nice girl."

He waits for her to answer, but Melanie only shrugs. He can think whatever he likes. She can be anything she wants in his car. Anything at all.

Milton flicks on the lights and throws his keys on a nearby table. Melanie wanders into his living room, drawn to the framed portraits hanging on the wall. He is a widower, he tells her, having survived two wives. Their portraits flank his own; they hang above an old TV against the center wall. The women aren't identical, but their ample figures and full faces that are more handsome than pretty make them look like kin. Melanie feels slight in their presence. They remind her of Bernice.

"You hungry?"

Melanie shakes her head.

"You should eat something. Put some meat on your bones."

Melanie smiles at his concern, thinks it is his way of covering his nervousness. She will have something, just for company. She follows him into the kitchen and sits at the table.

Milton microwaves leftovers, some sort of stewed chicken that Melanie thinks too spicy. "What's *insolence*?" she asks, to hide the fact that she is not eating.

He answers, "Girls like you."

"I'm serious."

"So am I. You call your mother by her first name and you run with strangers. You're probably worrying her to death right now."

Melanie doesn't bother to respond. It is still early in the afternoon; there is no reason for Bernice to be worried. She is easy to fool. Melanie doesn't tell him that she has sworn never to become her mother.

No one ever calls for Bernice anymore, but Melanie remembers the visitors. Men who wore suits with hats to match, transplants from the South like Bernice. These men dropped the names of old acquaintances Bernice had known back home and pretended they were just dropping in to check on her. They sat by Bernice's side as close as they could, watching her as if they were hungry and could never eat enough. Melanie would hide in the kitchen and spy, angry when Bernice brushed off their compliments and missed the meaning behind their words, angry that her mother had the power but foolishly refused to wield it. The way Melanie saw it, Bernice had thrown all of her chances away.

"We don't need to talk about my mother," she says.

Melanie finds his bedroom on her own. She doesn't wait for him to follow. She goes to it, undresses, peels back thin cotton sheets and climbs into his bed. What courtesy he shows when he turns his back to her while he undresses, before climbing in beside her. He doesn't pounce on her the way a boy her own age would. His legs are wiry and strong against hers, his feet bony and cold. How gentle it is when he parts her legs, how silent when he enters her.

Melanie lies next to his sleeping body, thinking that she'll have to work hard to keep her affair a secret. She'll make Milton park around the corner when he comes for her. She won't give him her phone number. She'll have to think of something to tell Chandra. Bernice, of course, can never know.

Melanie turns onto her side, curving against his back, resting her cheek against his shoulderblade. She was right to tell Chandra that boys their own age were immature. Milton seems to know about things she has never even thought of. He will take care of her, make her feel welcomed, cherished, loved. Here she is his woman, but as soon as she leaves, she will be just Melanie again, lost and needful. "Not yet," she whispers, wrapping her arms around his back.

Bernice is in the kitchen, paring apples for pie, when Melanie comes home. Melanie thinks her mother should know it at once. That it should be obvious. A difference in her walk and her bearing. She thinks there is now an air about her that exudes *woman*. But her mother is blind to it. Bernice drops an apple core into the trash and greets her, noticing nothing.

some other kind
of happiness

No one holds the syringe but me. My mother could if she weren't so squeamish about blood. There was a time when my cousin Tony could have learned to, but he came home to Brooklyn that summer a stranger. He'd been away all year at a boarding school in Connecticut none of us had ever seen. This left only Teddy, and even a blind woman could have seen that he coveted the hypodermic for his own.

Teddy, my grandmother's youngest son, and his newest girlfriend, Karen, were at the kitchen table playing backgammon.

"What you doing?" Teddy asked.

"Nothing." I opened the refrigerator door and bottles of cloudy insulin jostled in the built-in depressions meant for holding eggs.

"You about to give it to her?"

"Throw the dice," Karen said. "It's your turn."

"Want me to help?" he asked.

"No thanks," I said, warming a bottle of insulin between my

palms. "How long you all gonna be in here? I gotta clean the kitchen soon."

"I still say you're too young to be doing this," he said, shaking the leather dice cup. "You could accidentally stick yourself and get hurt. You don't even know what you're doing."

"I'm real careful," I said, willing to say anything to keep him away from us.

My grandmother waited in the back bedroom, watching soap operas until time for her injection. She kept the box of syringes in the top drawer of her bureau so no one could get to it without going across her bed. She removed one from the box and handed it to me.

Giving her the needle has taught me to be patient and gentle. You need to be in order to handle someone else's flesh. Daily handling has taught me well. I have been giving my grandmother her insulin twice a day for over a year now; I know her skin better than my own. I know when to move on before her skin gets sore; I know when to let her skin lie fallow. The outer upper arm, where even the most toned woman jiggles, is the best spot. There is always enough there to grasp, always extra meat to cushion the needle's prick.

"This won't hurt," I whispered, talking to her arm and not her. I pushed my grandmother's short sleeve up her arm and held a piece of flesh. "Don't you worry. This won't hurt a bit."

I swabbed the skin with alcohol. By now Teddy was in the doorway, watching, eyeing the syringe as I pulled the orange cap off and filled the hypodermic with insulin.

"What you want?" I asked him.

"I don't have to want nothing," he said. "I'm in my mama's room, in my mama's house."

Teddy moved in with us more than a year before Tony went away to school. After his previous girlfriend kicked him out, Teddy ended up outside our door, begging for a place to stay just until he could get himself back on his own two feet. His mother, my grandmother, was the only one who would take him in. No one else in our family trusted him; his older brother, Ralph, had stolen from too many family members to support his habit, and our relatives were wary that Teddy would do the same. He was given Tony's room to share and in Tony's absence he had painted it electric blue and hung his ten-speed bike from the ceiling. He showed no signs of getting back on his own two feet or of leaving anytime soon.

"Now cut it out you two," my grandmother said. "This baby's got to concentrate. Don't want her to give me the wrong amount."

"Gram, you know I wouldn't do that," I said, wounded.

My grandmother patted my hand. "I know, I know," she said.

"But she could, Mama. You could go into some kind of shock or diabetic coma or something. Naima could send you right into the hospital."

"You shut up!" I screamed.

"Ain't nobody going to no hospital today," my grandmother said. "If you're going to talk that kind of talk, you can leave us in peace. I don't need to be riled up before my shot."

"Sorry, Mama. All I'm saying is that it's better if more than one person knows how to give you your needle, that's all. No harm done. That's all I came to say. After all, Naima could go away to a school just like Tony. Then where would you be?"

"I'm not going nowhere," I said. We all knew this was true. Tony had been selected in junior high school to get a scholarship for that fancy school and to start in ninth grade. The only reason he had to wait was because Ralph filled out the paperwork incorrectly. Unlike Tony, I was not gifted. In my twelve and a half years, I had shown no extraordinary academic talent. Giving the needle was the only thing at which I excelled. I didn't have Tony's smarts or his prospects. I had nowhere to go.

Teddy backed away from the door, but his eyes never wavered

from the syringe. Occasionally, he scratched his arm, but his eyes followed my every motion as I pulled the plunger down to the appropriate line, tapped the syringe to release any harmful air bubbles, and glided the needle into the tautly held skin. After the injection, he disappeared silently and closed the door behind him.

When he was gone, my grandmother said, "Baby, he's got a point."

"What point?" I pulled the needle out. I pressed the sharp point against her bureau until it bent, then squeezed the cap back on.

"I can't expect you to do this all of the time. You're becoming a young woman and soon you'll have other things to do than sit around and play nursemaid to your old grandmother."

"I don't mind," I said. Before I began to give her the shots, my grandmother injected her insulin into her belly, her stomach the only fatty area she could reach. I'd see her sitting on the edge of the bed, trying to lift her dress out of the way with one hand and hold a section of flesh and inject herself all at once. In the year that I have been helping, I have come to love the slim little needles with their orange caps, the short and squat bottles of insulin, the perfect squares of alcohol prep pads. Teddy and Karen had their drugs; Tony had his away school; my mother had her cigarettes and her dates; my grandmother had her *All My Children* and *One Life to Live*; and I had this.

Tony was lying on one of his and Teddy's high-riser beds when I knocked on his bedroom door.

"What you doing?"

"Chilling," he said. Before he'd left Brooklyn to go away to school, he had pronounced that word the way we all did, by dropping the final *g*. Now it sat there on the end of his words, making him sound foreign to me. When I closed my eyes and listened to him, he sounded like the white boys on TV. He had become a person I could no longer speak to, could no longer recognize. He had come home sneering at us and our ways; the fancy school he had left us for had changed him. No one saw it but me, but there it was—a new, subtle way he had of now carrying himself, as if impatient to be away from us.

Some days he'd lie around the house in just his undershirt, shorts, and socks, cooling out under the fan, and no one was allowed to disturb him. Other days he was out the door as soon as he finished breakfast. He'd remain in the streets all day playing handball at the court in the park, returning for dinner, browned and sweaty. Every night, as soon as the sun went down and it became cool enough for folks to be sociable, Tony went out into the night, searching for the friends he'd left behind. He used these nights to shore up the gaps his absence during the school year had caused. Each night, as I watched him head out the door, I felt his desperation. He was *working* to have fun, gorging himself on his surroundings, burning the candle at both ends, trying to prove he had not lost his footing in his old world.

"Is that what you going to be doing all day?"

"Looks like it," he said. Though he was old enough to have his working papers, he had not bothered to get them. Long before he'd gone away, Tony talked about getting a summer job as a counselor in the recreation center so that he could be around the pool. He wanted to be a lifeguard, but he could not swim. Neither of us could. Three years ago, my mother took us to a class, but all we learned was to dunk our faces in the water and blow bubbles. "Why do you ask?"

" 'Cause we gotta clean the kitchen," I told him.

He rolled onto his side, lifting an underarm toward the oscillating fan. "Have to," he said. "Don't say 'gotta.' It's better if you say 'have to.' We have to clean the kitchen."

"Okay," I said. "We have to clean the kitchen."

"*I* don't have to," he said. "I'm home on break." He turned onto his back and folded his hands behind his head. While away, he'd grown an Afro. Now, he adjusted himself so that his head was directly in front of the fan. Every time it circulated back to him, it ruffled the edges of his Afro.

"Ma, Tony won't help me do the kitchen." Lying on our bed on her stomach, propped by her elbows, my mother was just inches away from the small black-and-white TV as she squinted through the zigzagged picture and tried to make out Diahann Carroll and James Earl Jones in *Claudine*. "Ma?"

"Let him be," she said.

"But he never do nothing."

"He's only home for a little time. It should be special," she said.

"He got the whole summer!"

"It's not a lot when you think about it. He's here for the whole summer, but gone the rest of the time." My mother inhaled on her cigarette, then held it out to me. "Go light this."

I plucked the cigarette from her fingers and took it to the kitchen. After three clicks, the right front burner came on and I lit the cigarette in the flame. When Teddy and Karen weren't looking, I sucked hard on the cigarette, inhaling the life of my mother. I was not yet bold enough to sneak a whole one; I took only drags whenever she sent me to light them. These short sweet stolen puffs, infrequent as they came, mellowed me as the smoke's effects swirled to the pit of my stomach and warmed my throat along the way.

I brought the cigarette back to my mother. She dangled it from her lips. "Come and fix this. You have the touch."

I slid my fingers up the TV's cold antennae, adjusting the rabbit ears carefully, moving each only a hairsbreadth at a time, indifferent to her directions. Just like there is a trick to giving a needle, there is a trick to fixing things. A trick of the touch. I touched the antennae one last time and Diahann Carroll appeared on the screen.

My mother said, "Don't be on Tony all the time. You know he's special. We have to do what we can to help him. We have to make sacrifices."

"Seem like that's all we do."

When Tony was a baby, my mother took him from Ralph and his girlfriend, sacrificing her youth to raise him right. While he was studying for his battery of tests and interviews, I sacrificed for him, too, washing and ironing his clothes and taking out the garbage when it was his turn. Now that he'd won, I wanted him to do his share, but it seemed that I would spend the summer doing both his chores and mine.

"Don't be like that," my mother said. "We can't stand in his way when he has a real chance to make it."

"Make what?" On screen, Diahann Carroll and her children scrambled around their dingy apartment, trying to hide the small appliances James Earl Jones had brought them before the welfare lady arrived.

"Make it out of here," she said. "He don't have to live like we do. He won't have to stay in nobody's projects. My baby's going to end up in the penthouse! And he'll be bringing us all along with him."

"What if I don't want to live in a penthouse?" My mother looked at me as if I had grown another head. Maybe it was the way she called Tony her baby even though he was her nephew and not her real son at all. Maybe it was the way she pinned all of her hopes and dreams on his brain, leaving no room for me to have a chance at saving our family. Maybe it was the way she, like him, sneered at our life, talking about leaving the projects as if it were an easy thing to just pick up and leave the only life I'd ever known.

My mother said, "He deserves a chance to find some kind of happiness, you know."

"Other than this?" I had thought we were happy.

She flicked a long line of ash into her ashtray and looked at me the way teachers do when you fall behind the rest of the class. "Some other kind of happiness, baby."

The next day, Teddy knocked on my grandmother's bedroom door while I was preparing her injection. Everyone knew I didn't like to be disturbed when giving the needle. Any distraction and I could miss an air bubble. "Hold on," I shouted.

"Can't," he moaned. "I can't hold on, you hear me?"

My grandmother said, "Let him in."

"When I'm done."

"Let my son in this room," she commanded. "Now."

I laid the insulin and syringe down and went to the door. "We're busy," I said, standing between him and the entrance.

"I'm sick," Teddy moaned. He stood at the door, his eyes vacant and hollowed.

He seemed as if he could barely stand. I couldn't see anything wrong with him, no cuts or bruises, and yet sickness radiated from him, a palpable thing. He looked past me to where my grandmother sat on the edge of the bed. "Mama!" He stumbled into the room and headed over to the bed. He shivered and wrapped his arms around his waist so tightly he looked as if he was wearing a straitjacket.

"Teddy, what is it?"

He crawled across the bed and wiggled his head onto her lap. He looked up at her with a look I had never seen before. She lowered her head to him and stroked his forehead and cheek. The two of them like that reminded me of something I'd once seen on a church's stained-glass window.

He gazed at her and pleaded, "Mama, I need some money real bad."

"I ain't made of money, Teddy."

"I know, Mama. I only need a real little bit." He sniffed and wiped his runny nose.

"Ain't it enough that I let you stay in my home and give you a roof over your head even though you're a fully grown man and I don't ask you for a drop of rent money?"

"You always been good to me, Ma," he said. "But I feel so bad."

My grandmother faltered. "You need the money for medicine or something like that?" she asked.

"Yeah, Ma," Teddy said, fidgeting beneath her steady hand. "Something like that."

My grandmother helped him off her lap. She turned to her bureau and rummaged through the top drawer for her change purse where bills were folded into thick squares. She pulled two squares of money out and unfolded them, pressing them out on the bureau's counter. "Will this help?"

Teddy took the money without looking at it. "Yeah."

After he'd gone, I resumed my preparations for the injection. I laid out the alcohol pads and the insulin, but the syringe I had placed on the bed had gone missing.

"Gram, do you see the needle anywhere?" I asked, warming the bottle of insulin in my hands. She checked the blanket to see if the syringe had rolled under a fold, but her search came up empty.

"It must've fallen," my grandmother said. She handed me another one from the box. I filled the syringe and flicked a finger against it to release the air bubbles. I took her flesh between my fingers and swabbed it with the alcohol pad, eager, wanting to pierce the too-trusting part of her the way needle pierced skin.

"This won't hurt," I whispered to the skin I knew.

She braced herself and I injected the needle. After I pulled it out, a single drop of blood surfaced on her skin. A small and perfect bubble, trembling between us two.

held

Kim knew better than to ask for a favor while her mother's shows
were on. Her mother sat on the love seat, positioned directly in
front of the TV, with newspaper spread out across her lap. She was
peeling potatoes to make french fries, routinely dropping peelings
onto the newspaper without ever looking at her hands or the knife.
She kept her eyes glued on the television, watching *Hawaii Five-O*.
She ignored Kim. When Kim crossed in front of the TV, her mother
didn't even blink. All she said was, "You not made of glass."

"Ma, please?" Kim whined. "She's your only granddaughter."

Kim's mother turned to face her. She was still young. Thirty-five.
But she was the mother of three and her face showed it. "Don't even
look at me like that," her mother said. "I already told you no. Don't
make me repeat myself."

Ever since she'd had the baby, Kim had been expecting something
different from her own mother. Something more along the lines of
guidance and advice. She expected her mother to give her pointers
and tips, to provide free babysitting, to help her along as if she was

an apprentice learning under a master. She hadn't expected the quiet censure her mother gave off without trying, the way she prefaced everything she said to Kim with "Now that you're a mother" or "Now that you think you grown." That was before she realized that her mother was most likely just jealous of her. After all, she had gotten her figure back quickly and naturally without having to exercise. She had rubbed cocoa butter onto her swollen belly every day of her pregnancy once her friend told her about it, and now she had no stretch marks. Kim had seen her mother walking around the house in a bra and slip, had seen the light brown streaks across her stomach stretching like a hand upwards towards her breasts. No wonder she was jealous.

A loud cry came from the bedroom Kim shared with her younger sister.

Her mother looked past her to the television and said, "You better go see to the baby. I don't know why you left her alone in there with only Asha anyway."

Kim didn't run; the baby was always crying and it was never over anything important. She crossed the crowded bedroom, walking past the two twin beds and toward the baby's crib, stepping over Asha, who was lying on the floor reading comic books, oblivious. "What happened?" Kim asked her. "What'd you do?"

"Nothing." Asha looked up from her comic book. She had the look of her father about her, deep brown skin and owlish eyes. "What did Ma say?"

"What you think?"

"Told you."

"Shut up." Kim looked down at the baby. She was lying on her back, staring up at Kim as she cried, naked except for her diaper.

"When are you gonna do my hair?" Asha asked. Her thick hair was wild around her head, making her look like she'd just woken up.

"Later."

"You already said that twice today."

"I'm saying it again," Kim said, looking down at the baby without really seeing her, her eyes blurring with tears. Let either of her two sisters need something, and her mother would no doubt break her neck falling all over herself. But let Kim ask for one little thing, and all of a sudden it was a federal case. "Why she gotta be like that?" she whispered.

"Who?" Asha asked. "Be like what?"

"Mind your business," Kim said. "Does she need to be changed?"

Asha shrugged, turning the page. "Do I look like her nanny?"

"Don't get smart." Kim rolled her eyes. She couldn't figure out how such a small infant could be so loud. She reached into the crib and tugged gently on the baby's fat brown leg. "Come on, now. Stop crying," she begged the infant. "Shush, baby. Hush now for Mommy?"

"I'm trying to read here," Asha said.

"Shut up," Kim snapped, checking the baby to see if maybe she was wet. The baby was dry and well fed. Kim didn't know why she got like this, why she cried for no reason. And she didn't know what to do to make her stop.

"What's the matter with Mommy's baby?" she asked, annoyed at how babies seemed to cry for no reason at all. There were many nights when the baby cried and Kim didn't go to her. She would just lie on the bottom of the bunk, listening to Asha snore and the baby cry. If Asha didn't wake up and complain, then Kim would let the baby go on until she got tired of crying and her breath got all huffed out like crying was a hard day's work. Asha would usually wake up by then. She would kick her foot against the mattress over Kim's head and say, "Can't you hear? You better get up."

And Kim would say, "Let her go on. She'll tire herself out."

Then Asha would kick some more and say, "I'ma tell Ma."

Kim would get up then because Asha was the youngest daughter, the baby of the family, and the apple of their mother's eye. Kim was only the middle child and not even the smart one—that was her older sister, Rashida.

Just when Kim's sleep would start getting good the baby would start crying to wake her up, uncaring that it was the middle of the night. The baby acted as if she was the only one that mattered. No one or nothing counted but her. Kim was sure she did it on purpose, just to prove she could.

On the nights when Kim did get up, the baby wouldn't even be wet or hungry. As soon as Kim peered over into the crib at her, the baby would stop and smile while her brown eyes were saying, *Look what I can make you do.* Neither Kim's mother nor her sisters had ever told her that babies were sneaky that way.

Kim rummaged around the crib and found the pacifier bundled up in the thin cotton blanket. She rubbed the lint off of it and tried to stick it in the baby's mouth, but she wouldn't take it. The baby cried with her mouth open so wide that Kim could see the back of her throat. Kim decided to be firm with her. "You gotta stop this noise right now," she said, but the baby continued.

"I hope she get laryngitis," Asha muttered, trying to turn her pages as loudly as possible.

"You be quiet," Kim said. "Nobody asked you."

Kim wondered if what Asha said was true, if the baby really could cry her voice away. "Please don't do that," she whispered so that Asha wouldn't hear. "Just stop crying for a minute. Just one minute, okay, please?" She took her daughter out of the crib and bounced her on her knee to see if that would work. The child stopped for a moment, then began anew in another fresh bout of squalling.

Asha said, "Maybe she's hungry."

"I already fed her. I did everything. Fed her. Burped her. Changed her. It's like she don't never stop." Kim looked at her daughter. "You don't never stop, do you?"

"If she answer you, I'm calling *Ripley's Believe It or Not!*" Asha said, no help at all to anyone.

Kim took the baby down the hallway and called to her mother.

"Ma! What am I supposed to do?"

Her mother shouted from the living room, "I know you not asking me nothing. You ain't want my advice this time last year, don't ask me nothing now." Then she turned the volume of the TV up louder to drown out the crying. The show was ending. Kim heard McGarrett say, "Book 'em, Danno. Murder one."

"Ma, can't you just watch her for two hours? Just this once? Please?"

"Two hours here, two hours there. Next thing you know I'll be running a day care center. I already raised my kids," she said.

"Yeah. What a fine job," Kim muttered.

"And don't think I can't hear you!" her mother shouted back.

"Dang. Don't have a heart attack," Kim said softly, making sure her mother couldn't hear this time. Why did it always have to be a federal case when she asked her mother to watch the baby?

Kim brought the baby back into her bedroom and put her into the crib. She retrieved the pacifier and forced it into the baby's mouth. Then she curled her hair and changed her clothes for the third time, switching from her cutoff denim shorts to a tight skirt and a shirt that left her stomach bare, glad that her old clothes finally fit her right. She looked at her watch and wondered if she would ever be able to get out of the house today.

None of her girlfriends had this problem. Their mothers were always willing to help out. They were supportive. But no, she had to live with a bunch of selfish people. Ever since she had the baby she hardly ever went out. By the time she'd dressed the baby and combed her hair just so, something would come up. Or if she actually made it out the door, little Danielle would cry or fuss or spit up before Kim could even get three blocks and she'd have to bring her right back. Kim's sister Asha was too young to watch the baby and Rashida was always too busy studying for her CUNY courses. And whenever someone did take the baby off her hands, they acted like they were doing her a favor. Like she should bow down and kiss the ground they walked on. They tried to make her feel bad every time she left the house, as if she was abandoning the baby. Like she was wrong to want to go and see Malik. Was she out of line to still want to go out and have some fun every now and then? They acted like she was dead and buried. No one wanted to help her. No one wanted her to have any fun. She was only sixteen.

Asha lifted her head up. "Rashida can watch her when she gets home."

"What you think I'm waiting for?" Kim snapped.

Asha rolled her eyes and reached for another comic book. She had a stack of them at her left elbow. She spent all of the money their mother gave her buying comic books. She could sit still for hours reading about the Riverdale High gang. Kim couldn't understand why someone would want to be cooped up all day reading about fake people when you could be outside with real ones.

Rashida was a bookworm, too. Only she didn't read comic books. She read thick textbooks with words so small they gave Kim a headache just to see them. Rashida worked part-time and took classes at the city college. She talked numbers—balance sheets and income statements and journal entries—she wanted to be an accountant. She was the only person Kim knew taking courses during the summer. The girls Kim's age went to summer school because they had to and most of the older girls that were Rashida's age had jobs. Rashida said it would help her get her degree faster. Kim thought it was a waste of both a good summer and good looks. Kim had never seen Rashida with a boyfriend and she blamed it all on her sister's attitude and not her looks. She was pretty without having to do much, but she wouldn't take advantage of it. When the two of them went out to the supermarket or to the pizza shop, the boys watched Rashida and spoke to her, but she never answered. When cars honked at her, she pretended not to hear. Unlike Kim, she never slowed her walk to a saunter or smiled out of the corner of her mouth. Kim secretly believed that Rashida was a twenty-year-old virgin.

Kim pulled a folding chair up to the window so that she could keep an eye on what was going on outside. It was still early enough in the day that only children and old folks were outside. Harsh sunlight glinted off the awnings of the corner store across the street. Young girls with strollers walked to the park. Boys in baggy jeans despite the heat guarded the corners and pay phones. The sun rocked off of the brown bricks of her housing project. She looked down below. A boy was riding a bike, his father chasing behind him, holding the training wheels in one hand. Four girls formed a square, clapping their hands against each other and singing:

> *We're going to Kentucky*
> *We're going to the fair*
> *To see the señorita*
> *With flowers in her hair*
> *Oh shake it shake it shake it*
> *Shake it if you can*
> *Shake it like a milkshake*
> *And do the best you can*
> *Oh rumble to the bottom*
> *Rumble to the top*
> *Then turn around and turn around*
> *Until you make a stop!*

Kids her own age weren't there. They were out working their summer jobs. Or they were taking care of their children. Or they were at the park. A girl from upstairs was sitting outside on one of the benches, braiding her boyfriend's hair. At nighttime, the courtyard would be filled with kids Kim's own age. Her mother would complain about the noise and say she couldn't sleep. Rashida would say she couldn't study. But Kim would love it. At night, they brought the music out. It was always like a block party with everyone outside chilling, joking, laughing, flirting, enjoying the coolness of a breeze in the few hours they had to cool down and kick back and be real before having to start all over again tomorrow.

The baby began to cry insistently. Kim went to the crib and tapped the mobile, hoping to create a distraction. Then she heard the front door unlock.

Kim didn't even let Rashida get halfway down the hallway before she grabbed her. "Your niece misses you," she said.

"Where is she?"

Kim nodded in the direction of her bedroom.

Rashida shook her head. She dropped her heavy book bag in the hallway and followed Kim into the room. She reached down into the crib and tickled the baby's stomach. "Hey, good looking."

"Hey," Kim answered.

"Not you. The baby."

"You know you're my favorite sister, right?" Kim said.

"What about me?" Asha said.

"Be quiet!" Kim hissed.

Rashida said, "I don't have any money."

"No, not money. I just need you to watch her for a little while. I gotta go see Malik." Just then, a fresh bout of crying began.

Rashida said, "I've got an accounting test tomorrow morning."

"It's not going to take long," Kim said. "I'm just going over there to get some money."

"How long?"

"Forever!" Asha piped in.

"Be quiet!" both Kim and Rashida said.

"Like two hours."

"Just some money?" Rashida held her gaze. "Why is she crying? Is she wet?"

"No she ain't wet. You think I don't know if she wet?" Kim said.

"Let me hold her." Rashida reached for the baby. She smiled at the baby and rubbed noses with her. "Hey Danielle. Hey pretty brown eyes," she sang as the baby gurgled, then grew quiet.

"How'd you do that?" Kim asked, awed.

"I didn't *do* anything."

"Maybe I can start singing like that to keep her quiet."

"You could just hold her," Rashida said. "Maybe you should give it a try."

It was just the type of thing she expected Rashida to say. Rashida would pop up with things out of the blue. She had a knack for saying things that had nothing to do with the conversation at hand. And their mother called Rashida the smart one.

"I ain't trying to raise no spoiled brat," Kim said. "I can't be holding her all the time."

"I'm not saying for you to pick her up every minute of the day, but sometimes you should just hold her so she knows she's loved and cared for."

"Can't nobody care for her more than I do," Kim said.

"I'm not talking about maintenance," Rashida said. Her voice took on that sad slow quality that it always did when she started explaining things. It made Kim feel like she was missing something important. It made her feel like a moron.

"How long has she been lying down?" Rashida asked.

"All day," Asha supplied.

"That's not true!" Kim argued.

"You never hold her," Rashida said. "I've hardly ever seen you do it."

"I do," Kim defended.

"Like when?"

"You want to know when?"

"When."

Kim couldn't think of a single time right off the top of her head, but she knew she could come up with plenty of examples if she had time to think. Besides, she spent plenty of time with the baby. She made sure to keep her hair brushed and oiled so that it would continue to grow. She kept her child clean. Now that it was summer and hot and sticky, she constantly made sure the child was covered in baby powder to keep her cool and dry. She didn't overfeed her. She was vigilant on diaper changing. She didn't see what else she could do.

"All of the time," Kim answered.

"Well then, she shouldn't be crying. She should be used to you holding her," Rashida said. She handed the baby back to Kim. "Here you go."

Kim snatched her baby back. She took the quieted child in her arms and smirked at her sister. "See? I hold her plenty." A moment later, the baby started to cry again. "Something must be wrong with her. She must be wet."

"You said she wasn't wet," Rashida said, shaking her head soberly.

"Well, maybe a tooth then. Anyway, she knows she's loved." She jiggled the crying baby. "You know you're loved, don't you?" she asked. Then she held the baby tighter and her voice became desperate. "Don't you?" she asked, shaking her.

She didn't like the way Rashida was watching her, or the way Asha was pretending not to. "I don't know why you think you can be all in my business, trying to tell me how to raise my child. Just 'cause I ask you a favor don't mean you all that. I didn't ask you for all that. I just asked you to look after her for like two hours, that's all. Dag. Think you better than somebody all the time. Forget it. I'll watch my own child. I don't need you or all of your advice."

Kim watched as her words made Rashida's face fall.

"I'm sorry," Rashida said, her eyes so round and full of wounded hurt that they reminded Kim of a deer. "I didn't mean to make you feel that way. I wasn't trying to usurp. I just don't want you to raise her like we were."

Kim knew what she meant. Their mother had barely raised them. Rashida woke them in the mornings and made them breakfast, getting out three bowls and pouring instant oatmeal and hot water into each one. All they needed to do was stir. Rashida sat them at the kitchen table and turned off the cartoons and made them do their schoolwork while she slid pans of french fries or fish sticks in the oven to bake or boiled a pot of rice. The one thing their mother did do was attempt to keep the house clean. But no matter how hard she tried, she couldn't do anything about the shabbiness. Crocheted doilies covered the coffee tables and the arms and backs of couches to hide their age. The sofa and matching love seat were old and worn; the turntable on their stereo set unit had been broken for over two years. They had three TVs, but only one worked. A nineteen-inch set sat on top of a floor model TV whose tube had blown and never been replaced. Kim didn't want her baby to grow up living like that.

"Yeah, well, you did usurp," Kim said, wondering what *usurp* meant. "And you don't have to worry about that. It'd be a cold day in hell before I ever raise my baby like that."

"If you say so."

"I do say so," Kim said. "Besides, you act like I'm a bad mother or something. I do everything I'm supposed to for her."

"Sometimes you have to do more than that," Rashida said.

"Oh?" Kim tightened her hold on the baby. "And how many children do you have?" she asked. Rashida swore somebody had died and made her an expert on every subject known to man, but for once, Kim could put her in her place. Kim waited for an answer. When Rashida didn't respond, she said, "I thought so."

Their mother came down the hallway and rapped on the door. "That baby still crying? What's going on in there?" she asked.

"Nothing," Kim said. She turned to Rashida. "So are you going to watch her or what?"

"All right. Just let me recopy my notes. Then I'll take her and you can go."

"You can study and watch her at the same time."

"No, I think I'll take her out to the park so she can get some fresh air. She likes that. You're not the only one who needs to get out every now and then," she said pointedly.

"Fine. Have fun. Don't blame me if you fail that test."

"I won't fail," Rashida said. She went back to her own room and closed the door to study.

"I won't fail," Kim mumbled in a snippy voice that she thought was a fair imitation of Rashida's. "I won't. No, not me. I never fail. I'm perfect. And I'm a better mother than you, Kim."

"Who are you talking to?" Asha asked when Kim came back in the room.

"Nobody."

"Are you about to leave?"

"Yeah."

"But you said you would braid my hair. I've been waiting for you all day."

"I'll do it later."

"What am I supposed to do until then? Walk around looking like this? You never come right back," Asha complained. Kim looked her over and felt sorry for her. Her hair was a mess. Asha must have washed it earlier in the day because it now stood out around her head in a tight tangled bush.

"Get the grease."

"It's finished."

"Then get the Vaseline."

When Asha came back with the Vaseline, Kim sat down on the edge of her bed and motioned for her little sister to position herself on the floor. Asha sat down between Kim's knees and leaned her head back so that Kim could line the part in her hair up with her nose to make it straight.

"It's not going to be nothing fancy now. I don't have time for all of that."

"I know," Asha said. "I just want you to do it and make it look nice."

"I don't have time to be making it look nice."

Kim began to part and grease sections of her sister's hair. Asha closed her eyes and said, "You always make it look nice."

Kim smiled and started to cornrow her sister's hair quickly upward into a high crown. It wasn't everyday that somebody gave her a compliment. Kim had never thought of Asha as attractive, but as she looked at her sister's smiling face, she saw the potential in Asha's good bone structure, thick brows, and curly lashes. If only she wouldn't stare at people all the time, guys might look at her twice. Maybe it was good that they didn't look at her. It meant that Asha had more time to herself. More time to read those silly comic books. The innocent and trusting ease on her face made Kim think her beautiful. She only hoped Asha stayed that way.

Kim paused at the front door before she left. Her mother was watching another show now. She had already peeled the potatoes. Now she was quartering them. Asha had already gone outside and Rashida was getting the baby ready for their trip to the park, and so it should have been easy to talk to her mother without the extra ears around. But it wasn't.

"You find somebody to watch her?" her mother asked without looking at her.

"Yeah." She started to leave. Then she turned back. "Ma?"

"Mmm?"

"Did you ever hold me?"

"What are you talking about?" she asked, looking up at Kim, her expression blank.

"I mean, when I was a baby, you know? Did you—did you used to pick me up a lot?"

"Well, you never cried a lot like your sisters. Never put up too much of a fuss—"

"I mean when I wasn't crying. When you didn't have a reason." Kim wanted to take her questions back and fly out the door. Even to her own ears, it sounded as if her life depended on the answer.

Her mother laid the knife down on the newspaper and smiled as if amused. "Yes, Kim I did hold you," she said. "I always had a reason. You were my baby. That was reason enough." When she said it and smiled as if in remembrance, with her head leaning to the side as if she was hearing a distant sound, Kim could see the pretty woman her mother had been before her kids and life had caught up to her.

Kim nodded. She felt silly for remaining in the doorway, yet she wanted to climb onto the couch. She wanted to be held again. She left the apartment quickly, knowing that if she remained she would only embarrass herself.

Kim got on the local and switched at Broadway East New York to the express. There was nowhere for her to sit on the train. She leaned against the doors, bracing herself, and read the same ads above the rail. Half of them were in Spanish. The other half were offers for invisible braces, good foot doctors, chiropractors, and legal attorneys offering to sue for malpractice. A Chinese man selling batteries, gum, and whistles moved through the car soliciting customers.

During the train ride, she made a mental promise not to get into a fight with Malik. She hated fighting in his tiny room with the thin walls, knowing that everyone in his house could hear. He wasn't a bad father. He loved to spoil the baby when he had the money. Already Danielle had two pairs of tiny gold earrings, one pair of small hoops and one pair of studs. She had a small gold bracelet. He'd even had her and the baby's name tattooed on his arm. But he was no good when it came to making steady payments or bringing routine supplies. He couldn't seem to figure out why one box of Pampers was not enough for the summer or seem to understand how fast a baby's feet could grow.

Malik kissed her and complimented her outfit. He led her past his siblings seated around the living room and drew her into his bedroom. He had a tiny box fan in his window; it hummed and blew hot air into the room. Before she sat down on the bed, Kim glanced at the mirror above his bureau. Taped to the upper left corner of it was a snapshot he had the nurses take of him, her, and the baby in the delivery room. Kim was holding the baby in her arms and Malik was leaning down beside her with an arm draped over her shoulder. Kim looked past the chubbiness of her oily face and focused on the way the three of them looked complete, like a real family, in that picture.

"I see you've still got that picture up," Kim said.

"My two ladies," Malik said. "Always." He showed off his right arm, flexing it for her, making the dark ink and cursive letters that were her and the baby's names jump. He always did it to make her laugh.

For a while, they talked as they listened to songs on the radio. He talked about work. Then he asked about the baby. He grunted when Kim told him about all the crying, but when she started to ask for money, he rolled over on the bed and closed his eyes. He said, "You're always coming over here for money."

"Where else I'm supposed to go?"

"Don't start, Kim."

"Why I gotta be starting when I ask you to take care of your daughter?"

He turned back around to face her. "You think I don't want to take care of her? Do you even see all the people living in this damn house? How you think they eat, Kim? How you think they pay the rent? How you think I get to stay here? I got to put money into this right here to make sure I got a roof over my head before I can go throw some money at you."

She hated how he did that, took her words and talked them into a way that made it seem like she was the selfish one. "She's your daughter," she said.

"I know that. And this is my family. If I say I ain't got it, I ain't got it. What, Kim? Do you think I got a stash of money lying around here and I'm hiding it from you? I ain't got it, and I wish you stop coming over here asking for shit I ain't got!"

She got off the bed. "Fine, then I won't come no more! You don't never have to worry about us!"

There were tears in her eyes that she didn't want him to see. She turned her head and smoothed out the creases in her skirt.

"Don't get like that," he said. Malik stood up and went to her. "But how you think I feel, knowing you coming on over here, knowing what you gonna ask me, knowing I got to say no again and have you look at me like I ain't shit?"

"I didn't say all that," she protested, sitting now on a corner of his bed, far away from him, tucking her hands under her thighs. "I just can't do it by myself." She could force him to pay. Her mother and sister had told her about her options. She could take him to court, garnish his checks, have him be ordered to pay child support. But then she would lose him. She'd have money coming in for her daughter, but Danielle would lose her father. If he felt all he had to do was pay, then that was all he would do. He wouldn't be in their lives. Kim had seen her friends take that route and the kids were the ones that really lost out. Besides, she didn't want any bad feelings between them. She hadn't thought about how it would make him feel to have to say no. She only knew what it felt like to hear it, then have to go back home and face the knowing eyes of her mother and sisters.

"We could get our own place," she whispered. "Then it would just be our bills. Nobody else's."

He didn't try to hide his amusement. "You not even eighteen. Can't put your name on nobody's lease."

Kim nodded. She bit her lip and fixed one of her curls that had begun to wilt.

"Look, can we just not think of this for a while?" he asked, tugging on her leg.

"No," Kim said. "I ain't come here for that."

"Okay." He took her hand and drew light circles on her palm. "Okay." Then he moved closer to her and began to kiss her until she forgot why she had originally come.

Kim got off the train and changed her mind about heading home. Without knowing she was going there, she found herself at the park.

Rashida was seated on a bench across from the kiddie swings reading out loud from a small white book. She held the baby on her lap; the stroller stood nearby. For once, the baby wasn't crying.

"Hi."

Rashida looked up from the book. "What are you doing here? Don't tell me that after all that Malik wasn't home?"

"He was there," Kim said. "I just came to get Danielle so you could study."

"I told you it was all right. I have my notes—"

"I just wanted her."

Rashida faltered for a moment, sitting stock still with the baby. Then she smiled brightly and said, "Hey. That's fine. I mean, she's yours, right? You can have her whenever you want." Rashida handed the baby over and gathered her belongings. As soon as Kim held her, the baby started to cry.

Now that she was alone with the child, Kim didn't know what to do. Most of the time, someone else was always around, watching her. Now the pressure was off of her for just a moment. No one was looking over her shoulder.

Kim changed the baby's position and held her under the arms, lifting her high. Kim wiggled her a little so that her tiny feet swung in the air. The crying stopped.

"You like that," Kim said. "Hey."

She realized that she was holding the baby incorrectly and brought her back down. She put her hands around the baby's waist and lifted her back into the air. She did it swiftly and the baby began to gurgle and make nonsense noises.

Kim brought the baby back down and held her out at arm's length so that she could look her over. All this time she had thought there was more of Malik in the child than herself. But now she could see traces of her features shining through. It was the eyes. They were hers. A dark, dark brown that made the pupils hard to see. There was a little bit of her in her daughter. She could see herself. Kim touched her daughter's cheek with a finger and smiled into the eyes that were like polished black mirrors.

The baby was quiet now, but curious. Rapt. Her eyes followed Kim's every movement. She brought the infant closer and inhaled, smelling the warm baby scent of powder and new, new skin. The baby reached for her hair and Kim laughed, feeling like the two of them were the only two people that had ever been in the world. And they were only now just meeting.

yearn

Kiki didn't have anything smaller than a twenty on him at lunch-time. He'd pulled out a roll of twenties and fifties and told Stephen to meet him at the park when school let out. Stephen had never seen so much money on someone his own age. And even though he knew he was supposed to head straight home, he agreed to meet at the park.

When he got there, he went straight to their spot, a stone house at the edge of the playground that all the kids called the White House. Stone turtles, dolphins, horses in midgallop were scattered all around the park, but the White House was where the boys played spider, where the couples did it, where the teenagers played handball, and where he and Kiki met.

That afternoon, they had it all to themselves.

"Look what I got." Kiki had a bag full of fireworks, Jumping Jacks, cherry bombs, Butterflies, Ashcans. It wasn't even the Fourth of July.

"Oh snap, where'd you get those? Did you go to Chinatown?"

Kiki was smug, "I got my ways, Steve. I even saw *The Spearman of Death*."

"For real? The one with the Five Deadly Venoms?"

"No, for fake, Mama's boy," Kiki pushed him and laughed.

"I'm not." But even to himself, it sounded whiny.

Stephen imagined Kiki—short, pudgy, and Puerto Rican—riding the subway up to Chinatown, buying fireworks and rice candy, and maybe even taking in a kung fu flick, a real one with the English badly dubbed over. He wished he could have gone. Just thinking about all the things that his mother kept him from doing got him upset. He was almost twelve and still being treated like a baby. If it weren't for Kiki, he'd never get to light any fireworks. His mother was too worried he'd blow his fingers off.

His mother was too worried about too many things. She was worried about where they lived. She didn't like Bed-Stuy. They lived on a block with nothing but brownstones. Even though they didn't live in the projects, she said it was still the ghetto. The boys that lived on the block and in the surrounding area worried her. The way they grew up and took up residence on the street corners and glued themselves to the pay phones, rigging them so no one else could use them. The way they wore their jeans so low that they seemed to hang off their narrow behinds. And the way they carried pagers and cell phones as if they were doctors and lawyers even though they had no jobs and nowhere to go. She worried that those boys or boys just like them would kill him. One day, she said, they would turn around and shoot him straight through the head if he said the wrong thing.

But he knew that she was wrong. The older boys were his friends. They looked out for him. She worried over nothing and made him look like a punk in the process.

"I'm not a mama's boy," Stephen said this time without whining. "I'm *not*."

"Be cool, Steve," Kiki said.

They started out behind the kiddie swings. Kiki pulled the Jumping Jacks out of their thin red paper and left the dozen twisted together. He lit the whole pack at once and they watched as it leapt into the air, each firecracker straining against another, ready to dance, each side fizzing and glowing orange, yellow, and green.

"Yo, that was fresh," Kiki said.

"You gonna waste them, doing them like that."

"It's plenty more where that came from. Chill out. Scaredy."

"I'm not!"

"Then follow me," Kiki said as they began to walk away, kicking paper bags and crack vials out of their path. Kiki stopped and watched a group of girls playing rope from a distance. "Isn't that that *puta* Maribel you tried to talk to?"

"Yeah, that's her," Stephen said, not sure what a *puta* was. She was playing double Dutch with two girls he didn't recognize. Her back was to him and he lost his train of thought for a moment as he watched her denim cutoffs sway back and forth to the rhythm of the rope she was turning.

"—a lot of nerve turning my boy down. I'll show her she can't play with my homie like that," Kiki was muttering. He reached around in his bag until he pulled out a stink bomb.

"Get behind that tree!" Kiki shouted as he lit and tossed the stink bomb at the girls and scampered out of sight.

"Yo, why'd you—"

Kiki was doubled over with laughter, "Stop frontin'. You know you thought that was funny."

He tried to deny it, but as soon as he opened his mouth, he started to laugh hard. It *had* been funny to watch the girls. They had started sniffing the air and before they'd realized it was a stink bomb, the girls had all stared at Maribel with disgust, as if the smell came from her. Red-faced, Maribel dropped her end of the rope and ran.

"Bet you wish you coulda did it yourself," Kiki said.

He wondered how Kiki knew. Stephen had tried to dance with Maribel at her birthday party twice and she'd turned him down. He'd written her a note, asking her to go steady with him and she'd shown it to all the girls in their class at lunchtime. When he'd seen the note wafting through the cafeteria, covered in chocolate milk stains, he *had* wished for some sort of divine hand to come down and smack her silly. But he hadn't done anything himself. It felt good to see her get humiliated for a change.

Kiki pulled himself together, "Damn, I almost pissed myself from that. Serves her stank ass right."

"Stank ass!" they both screamed with laughter.

They heard the Mister Softee ice cream truck a block away and Stephen realized he was late. The ice cream man always came down their block between five-thirty and six, when he judged the parents would be home to give their kids money. "Oh dip, I gotta go," he said.

Kiki gave him a pound, "I got a little more work to do first. I see that *pendeja* Rosario over by the swings. I got something for her."

"I thought that was your girl?"

"I dumped her. I started going with Tiffany yesterday. Come by my house tomorrow after school."

"I don't know. I'll try."

"She's bringing her girlfriend Wanda over. She'll heal your broken heart."

"Man, forget you," Stephen said. But as he walked away, he was trying to remember what he knew about Wanda. Wanda had started to grow real breasts in the fifth grade. He'd find a way to be there all right.

By the time he got to his street, MacDonough, everyone was already outside. He walked through the maze of bodies, sidestepping double

Dutch ropes that whipped by fast enough to sting and stepping over the boys using yellow chalk to etch their lines and numbers on the sidewalk so they could play skelly, without really seeing any of them. He could count on his neighbors to be the same. Each day the heat brought them downstairs with the promise of a breeze or two before dinner. The stoops were littered with adults playing cards, fixing hair, smoking, and talking. Each day the old men on the street congregated in front of 32, his building, and sat on milk crates at the top of the stoop, dressed for church and talking quietly to each other. And each day Miss Earlene drank herself into a stupor and tried to pick fights.

"Yes, that's what I said! These kids here today ain't amountin' to nothing." She looked up at the old men on the stoop for support but they ignored her. She sat at the bottom of the stoop, with her knees spread and her skirt tented over them, a forty-ounce bottle of beer in her lap. Stephen knew the moment she laid eyes on him.

"Not even close to nothing! Look at you. Yes, you Townsend boy. You, Stephen, you! You special, huh? That's what your mama make you out to be? What's your father say, huh? Mama's baby and Papa's maybe. Your daddy wasn't nothing and you ain't never gonna be nothing neither."

Miss Earlene was a conversational drunk. After a few beers she talked to any one who would listen. His mother said she had been beautiful once, when she was much younger. And what his mother hadn't told him, but others had, was that Miss Earlene had loved his father and tried to steal him away. She and his mother had gotten into fights over his father, and his grandmother always had to pull them apart.

He'd learned to ignore Miss Earlene's tirades over the years. Especially when they were about his father. All his mother had ever said was that his father had left them, and since Stephen had been too young to remember him, he'd left it at that. He had no feelings where his father was concerned. No hatred, no bitterness, no nothing. He was the only remainder of his father's presence. There were no pictures or souvenirs. Only absence. Drunk as she was, Miss Earlene was careful. She could say what she wanted about his father, but she knew better than to say anything about his mother.

The kitchen was hot because the windows were closed and the shades drawn; the smells that would have wafted out now turned back and circled around the apartment. His mother stood in front of the stove, her brown arms and elbows smattered with flour. Her short pixie haircut was wilting. Damp black tendrils framed her face. She was frying chicken when she heard him come up behind her.

"Hey, Ma."

"Hey, yourself. Where you been?"

"Out. Chillin'. You know."

"No, I don't know. That's why I asked you. Mind telling me why you didn't take out the garbage today? Too busy doing all your 'chillin'?"

"Ah, c'mon, man—"

"Boy, who are you talking to?"

"Ma, I forgot, all right?"

"Well, why don't you just go on and remember, then?"

"All right. Dag."

"Stephen, how many times I got to tell you to quit saying that? Sounds too much like damn."

"Sorry."

"Thank you." She kissed his cheek and wiped off the counter, motioning for him to help his grandmother set the table.

They sat down to eat and his mother opened up the conversation after saying grace, "You sure were late getting home today. I got here before you. What were you doing?"

"Nothin' really. Chillin'."

"Well, who were you doing 'nothing really' with?" she asked.

"Nobody."

"I may not be hip, Stephen, but even I know you can't 'chill' alone. I don't mind if you stay after to be with your friends as long as it wasn't that Kiki. But I know it wasn't Kiki because I told you I didn't want you around that rough little boy anymore. He's got too much time on his hands and too much money in his pockets for a boy that age."

"Does he have a rich grandfather, do you think? Maybe he could give me some of that money," his grandmother quipped.

Stephen bit back his laughter, "No Gram, he don't have no rich grandfather."

His mother raised her eyebrows and sent his grandmother a knowing look, as if he couldn't understand their communication. "Mama, that money is dirty money. He gets money from that brother of his," she said.

"Wilfredo has a job, Ma."

"Mmmhhm. A job. Washing cars down on Atlantic Avenue. They don't pay that kind of money down there. He got a job but he's got a something else, too," she said.

She wouldn't say the words *drug dealer*, but he heard them just the same.

"Ma, Kiki's brother is not what you think. It's nothing wrong with his money."

"First off, don't tell me what I think. You don't know where Wilfredo's money comes from and neither do I. I swear. One of these days, somebody gonna come looking for that boy to make him pay up and whoever is around him is gonna get caught up in it. Even if they're just minding their own business. And they gonna be real sorry, too. When they come looking for him, they're not gonna care who all is with him or if they're kin or if they're too young or what. Just don't let it be my child, please," his mother said, speaking to no one in particular but making it clear that she was talking to him. She wiped her mouth with a paper towel that had been folded to look like a napkin. When she put it down, he could see the faint traces of the raisin-colored lipstick she wore to work. "But none of that even matters since you don't play with Kiki anymore. Isn't that right, Stephen?"

He didn't answer.

"I said, isn't that right, Stephen?"

His grandmother jumped in. "Stephen, you hear your mama talking to you?"

He still didn't answer.

His mother pushed her plate away from her and started to stand but thought better of it. "Stephen, I have had enough of this. Now I am going to ask you this question one last time and this time you are going to give me an answer. Were you out again with Kiki?" She watched him closely, skewering him under her glare.

He shifted in his seat, "Yeah, Ma."

"I told you I don't want you hanging around with that boy!"

"But Ma, he's my boy. You can't—"

She slapped him across the face, "I don't want to hear another word! He's not *my* boy, you are, and I don't care what you say about him! You got another think coming if you expect me to put up with you disobeying me! And don't even think of stepping one foot outside this house tonight or any other night until I say so. Take yourself to your room this very minute or else I'm not gonna be responsible for what might happen if you stay in my sight. Lord, give me strength. And I better not hear no TV on in there and no video games! You hear me?"

He rose sullenly and left the table, dragging his feet, his face stinging.

All of their bedroom doors were closed to each other. Stephen was lying on his bed and listening to the sounds in the other two bedrooms. The music that his grandmother called the blues was playing in her room as it always was whenever she was alone in her room. His mother was behind the door in her own room, crying.

He often made his mother cry. But he was always sorry. And he had never made her cry like this. This time her crying was louder than the music in his grandmother's room. This time it sounded as if it would never stop. He opened her door and let a little bit of light slip through so that he could look at her. Lying across the bed on her stomach, she looked a C of sorrow with her back curved up and her face buried in her arms. He felt a little sick inside when he realized what he was doing to her. He felt as if he had eaten something bad and couldn't get the taste of it out of his mouth.

Hurting her wasn't something he did on purpose. It just seemed to always happen whenever he did the things he yearned to do. The two of them didn't see eye to eye on anything. She saw the danger, the trouble, before she saw anything else. Sometimes he wondered what kind of man his father had been. If he was the kind of man who took chances and saw the possibilities instead of the problems. He wondered if his father had seen his mother with her short pixie hair and lips dark as grapes and seen all the possibilities with her only to find out that she saw only pitfalls to be avoided, that she kept her feet rooted firmly to the ground and would not pick up and follow him wherever, that she would rather hear him tell her that the bills were paid on time than say she was beautiful. Stephen wondered if there was any of his father in him, if that was the difference that made everything so hard, if it was his father in him that his mother saw and worried over.

He didn't go to her. He let her cry. He had done this enough to know all the things that she would say:

> *These boys, they'll kill you.*
> *They'll take everything you have.*
> *They don't want you to have nothing.*

They see that you're smart. That you've got a little something go-ing for you. And they hate it. It makes them mad.

They'll smile at you now, but when you try to do something for yourself, when they see you trying to have a little something to your credit and name, they'll try and stop you.

Stephen, why you make it so hard?

If you could just listen sometimes. You're my baby, and I'm just trying to keep you alive.

He closed her door, standing there with his hand on the door-knob. He gripped the knob tightly until he could see his brown knuckles lighten with the strain of it. He wouldn't go in, but he listened long to the tears she was crying for him.

He went to his grandmother's room and knocked lightly on her door.

"Can I come in, Gram?"

"Yes, baby. Come on in." She was lost in thought, leaning out of her chair, bending over her record player. "Have a seat," she said.

He sat down on the floor by her feet and rested his head on her lap, comforted by the scent of peppermint balls in the pockets of her housedress. Her lap was warm. Her hand came down to rest on top of his head. She stroked his hair lightly.

"How you feelin', baby?"

"Okay, I guess." He didn't want to explain. He just wanted to sit there and feel the comfort of her old fingers slowly weaving in and out of his hair.

"You want me to rub your feet, Gram?" His grandmother was always complaining about having poor circulation in her legs and feet. Sometimes he had to help her put her knee socks and shoes on before her doctor's visits. Sometimes he had to rub the life back into the soles of her feet.

He knelt before her and braced her feet up on his thighs. He began to rub lotion on the cracks and hard, dead skin of her heels. The music came to him softly as he rubbed.

There ain't nothin I can do
Nothin I can say
That folks don't criticize me.

After a few minutes, she sighed. "Thank you, baby, but you don't need to be in here rubbing an old woman's feet. These feet done more walking than you can ever imagine."

He shrugged. "I don't mind, Gram. I know you're tired."

"Oh? Who told you?"

"I have my ways," he said, thinking of Kiki and his cryptic answers. "Like right now I know you're thinking about something." When she looked at him curiously, he jerked his head to the record player in response. The music had stopped but the needle continued to play and move, making shushing sounds on the record's edge.

" 'Cause you letting your record getting scratched up. The song's over." He got up and took the needle off the record. "Want me to play it again?"

"No baby, take the one off the top of the stack."

"But that one's scratched worse than this one."

"It'll play," she assured him.

He pulled the forty-five out of its paper sleeve and put it on. The needle scratched several times. Then it caught.

"Ah, now this is it." She leaned back. He recognized Billie Holiday's voice. His grandmother's favorite singer. His mother liked her, too. He could never forget Lady Day's voice. His mother said she and his father used to play Billie Holiday records to soothe him when he was teething and crying loud enough to wake the neighbors. He didn't remember any of that, but sometimes it did seem that her voice called to him when he was listening, that sometimes it was reaching just for him. She always sounded to him as if she was aching. He thought she sang as if her heart was torn at the seams.

That voice surrounded the two of them in the room.

Them that's got shall get
Them that's not shall lose.

He saw that when his grandmother closed her eyes, the fine lines around her eyes disappeared. He pressed both thumbs hard against her heel and rubbed. She said, "Can't for the life of me figure out why they wanna call this stuff jazz. Ain't nothing about this jazzy. Don't nothing in this music make you wanna get up, snap your fingers, put on a pretty dress and some red lipstick. Make you wanna be at home with your thoughts, know what I mean?"

So the Bible says
And it still is news.

"You know, your problem is you listen to the wrong people. You wanna be out there so bad, but it ain't nothing out there. Why you gonna listen to your friends over your family? That boy ain't done nothing to make you stay." She spoke as if her feelings were hurt. Her voice, coming after a long period of silence, startled him, and her words and tone sparked the need in him to defend himself, but he couldn't say anything without sounding fresh.

He wanted to pull down their way of life. To say that he didn't want to live quietly like they did, without a sound. To say that he needed someone like Kiki to keep him sane enough to live with them. But he knew better than to open his mouth and talk back. He held her leathery feet in the flesh of his hands and rubbed them back and forth, her toes cracking under the heels of his hands.

"Now that boy Kikuyu—"

"Kiki."

"Whoever. Does he work to feed you?"

"No, Gram. You know that."

"He save his dollars to buy you things, sneakers for your feet and food for your stomach? Money for all these fancy haircuts you always need, or these video games that's like life and death to you?"

"No, Gram."

"Then what is it? That boy don't never come over here or call on the phone like decent folks. He's always got to be sneaking around, hanging on street corners. What he do that you got to be out there all the time chasing after somebody that don't do nothing for you? Must be something."

Mama may have
Papa may have.

He couldn't tell her what Kiki did for him; he wasn't sure he understood it himself. Like today, Kiki did the things that he only thought of doing. Kiki made his thoughts real and put them into action. Kiki dared. And when he was with him, he dared, too.

"Well?" she prodded, but he knew better than to answer. She huffed in some air and told him to change the record.

"You just like your granddaddy," she said. This made him look up. His grandfather was a subject wrapped in tissue paper. No matter how lightly you touched it, it would rustle.

"How come?" But she wasn't listening. She was shaking her head in time to the music.

"He thought he knew everything there was to know 'bout life. Made me believe it, too. He got me to move up here to New York—did you know that?—just knowing it was gonna be different. But one place ain't no different from no place else. People try and make it like everything's new only to find that the devil done followed you wherever you move and all you can do is hold him off a little while whiles you catch your breath.

"People'll tell you this used to be a nice block. Way back when. When we settled up here, there wasn't as many of us as it is now, but ain't nothing different. What we doing now, the Jews and Italians who moved off done already been through. It might've been different folk, but things don't change. And he couldn't realize that. Thought a place was gonna change something. But if something in you ain't reconciled and you go somewhere else or be with somebody new, is it gonna be healed?"

This time she seemed to really want an answer. Her dark eyes held him in place, waiting. "No, ma'am," he mumbled, "I guess not."

He waited for her to pull out the lesson from her story, to tell him to heed his mother, expecting her to bring it all back somehow and make him feel guilty. But she just rocked to the record, and when it ended, he put the needle back to the beginning again. She began to sing with the record, her voice throaty, a low rasp.

But god bless the child that's got his own
That's got his own.

He set her feet down and shook his hands out. He got up from his chair and walked over to her small window. The shade was pulled all the way down. He knew he didn't need to lift it to see what waited for him outside.

The old men lined the stoops, their long legs hanging over the blue, red, and orange crates and down a step or two. They wore their best slacks, with the creases ironed in, as if they were going to work. Their backs stooped and bent, their hands hung down in the space between their legs, thin brown fingers laced loosely together. Beneath their Sunday hats, their eyes were sad, and when they spoke quietly among themselves, their voices came out rusty.

His grandfather could have been any one of them if he had lived.

His father could have been any of them—one day—if he had stayed.

Stephen never wanted to be like those men. Just once, he wanted to pull that shade up and not see them sitting there like always. He wanted his mother not to have to worry about him, not to have to cry.

The record ended and his grandmother was still singing, her body bent and nodding toward the record player.

Part of him wanted to stay right there at his grandmother's feet, to keep that window shade pulled all the way down so that not even a crack of light from the outside could show through. But another part wanted to tug the threaded cord quickly, sending the shade snapping up to the top, where it would roll on itself, flap, and break the silence. Because beyond his stoop, over the heads of the old men and past the edge of his block, the park was not empty. Kiki was still out there even though it had grown dark, shooting skyrockets that zipped and exploded into myriad colors in the night dark sky. He was setting off Moon Whistlers, which flared and pierced the heavy stagnant air; he was lighting and tossing Ashcans, which resounded like claps of thunder. Stephen moved to replace the needle and replay the record. He passed the window and lingered, straining to hear.

The Flannery O'Connor Award for Short Fiction

CPSIA information can be obtained
at www.ICGtesting.com
Printed in the USA
FSOW02n2015031016